Chapter One

London, October 1911

Owen Hadley reclined in a leather armchair in one of the gaming rooms of Brooks's club on St. James Street, a glass of brandy warming his hand as he glowered at the occupants of the room. It was late in the evening and many of the old regulars of Brooks were coming in for supper. Owen's attention was only partially on the young lords gambling away their fortunes. A scowl curved his lips down as he watched the coins and pound notes changing hands.

He was in bad need of money, and the irony was not that his need arose from any vice or fault of his own. At thirty-two he was the only male heir in his family, and his estate in the Cotswolds depended on him. While he'd be away fighting a war, the land and house had fallen into disrepair and the tenant farms had been abandoned. Only a large influx of money could bring it back to life. Money he didn't have. Being merely landed gentry, land was all he had, and his was hurting.

I need a wife.

As much as he was loathe to admit it, marrying an heiress would solve the problem. But finding a woman and getting approval from her father for the match would be difficult. There were many other men, impoverished peers who could offer young ladies and their families' titles as trade for their dowries. Owen grimaced. He could offer no titles, nothing else to persuade a lady to marry him. He glanced about the other tables in the club, misery darkening his mood further.

One of the young men nearby cheered as he won a winning hand. The temporary excitement in the tame quiet of the room was grating on Owen's ears. He scowled in the direction of the exuberant gamblers. The downward movement of his lips and the tensing of his cheeks caused a bolt of pain along his bruised jaw. One week ago, he'd caught a train down to Hampton House, the country residence of his close friend Leo Graham, the Earl of Hampton.

One of the house party guests had been a divine raven-haired creature named Ivy Leighton. Her father was the owner of a London newspaper. He was nice and more importantly he was rich. The possibility of seducing the

B.E.A

A Gentleman Never Surrenders

SINS AND SCANDALS
BOOK TWO

LAUREN SMITH

Cover design by Holly Perret

ISBN: 978-1-958196-91-5 (ebook)

ISBN: 978-1-958196-28-1 (print)

nouveau-riche newspaperman's daughter had been impossible to resist. A *very rich* young lady who would have set his home well up with her fortune. Owen had been so close to saving his estate, but he'd acted foolishly.

Perhaps a little *too* foolishly, he amended. Leo had gotten upset when he found Owen trying to steal a kiss from the young lady. Owen had been attempting to compromise her in the presence of witnesses. In such a situation, marriage would have been guaranteed, but Hampton had come upon them first and knocked Owen senseless. He still didn't understand why he and his friend, a man he'd never quarreled with before, had come to blows without warning over a woman. Owen had never felt strongly enough about any woman to throw a punch for her.

"Hadley?" A familiar voice disturbed him from his thoughts. He glanced up to see Leo staring at him with a mixture of amusement and irritation.

"Hampton," he replied, a tad gruff. He hadn't enjoyed his friend rendering him unconscious by snapping him a good blow to the jaw. It hadn't been too sporting to strike a man unawares, and Owen's pride stung a little.

"I'm glad you're here. It's been ages since we enjoyed a night at the club—"

"What do you want?" Owen growled.

"I'm sorry. I suppose I owe you an apology for hitting you. But damnation, Owen, you were in the wrong."

Owen shot him a challenging glare. "Why did you hit me? I was trying to secure myself a wife. Ms. Leighton would have been perfect for me."

"I couldn't let you have her—Ivy, I mean." Hampton lowered his voice. Speaking of a lady, even in good terms, in a club was taboo. Owen didn't care for such rules, but Leo was more of a gentleman. Ever since they were lads, Owen had always been the one more likely to get into trouble.

"Why not? Are you...interested in her?" Owen prodded, sensing there was a change in his friend. Leo seemed more...alive, like the old Leo he'd been before his father had died and the responsibilities of the estate crushed all the fun out of him.

"We were childhood friends. I hadn't seen her since she was eight, and when I met up with her again...I fell for her, *hard*. She's agreed to marry me." Leo's cheeks turned a ruddy red as he admitted this, and Owen would have laughed under other, less-tense circumstances.

So Leo was marrying the heiress? Lucky devil. *But I'm the one who really needed her.*

"I see." Owen sat back in his chair, which was close to the wall near the electric bell. He rang it and waited for the attendant. If he and Leo were going to have a discussion involving women, he needed a stiff drink.

"I should have declared my intentions toward her, Hadley. I would have, but damned if I didn't know what my intentions were until I saw you with her." Leo eased into a chair opposite Owen and nodded toward the bruised spot on Owen's face. "I'm sorry about that."

Owen's annoyance with his friend was temporarily weakened.

"I hope we can go on as we were before?" Leo inquired, his tone still low, careful. Leo was always so bloody cautious. Except when it came to Ivy Leighton, apparently. After Leo's unexpected show of violence, Owen hadn't stayed at Hampton House. He'd run back to London like a kicked dog with his tail between his legs. But their friendship ran river deep and he was not about to let a quarrel over a woman destroy that bond.

"Of course," he reassured his friend. "You can make it up to me by finding me a rich wife," he half jested, but Leo saw through the sardonic air he'd usually cloaked his troubles with.

A servant came over with a decanter and refilled Owen's glass before offering Leo his own drink, which he accepted gratefully. After the servant left, Leo shot him a meaningful look.

Leo inched closer. "It's Wesden Heath, isn't it?"

Rather than reply, he nodded. The state of his home's affairs was dire, and thinking of it turned his stomach. And he didn't want to keep discussing his crumbling estate with his friend.

"Perhaps I can help you there. Ivy and I will be

hosting another house party soon, for a Scottish lord Mother knows, someone related to her cousin I believe. Would you consider coming back for it? The Pepperwirths have just allowed their youngest daughter, Miss Rowena, to have her come-out. She's a lovely creature. Eighteen and a sizeable dowry. I know you'd do well by a wife, Hadley, so you might have a chance with her. Perhaps, if you play your hand right..." Leo trailed off, letting Owen pick up on his unspoken suggestion.

Owen sat up, confused. "Mildred Pepperwirth has a little sister?" He nearly laughed, which would have been the height of rudeness. Mildred was the eldest daughter of Viscount Pepperwirth, whose lands abutted Leo's to the west. She was a beauty, but cold and lacking in personality and warmth. The woman didn't even dance, for heaven's sake. Owen loved a woman who danced, who laughed and smiled. A woman should be happy; she should be brilliant and witty, not a cold shrew. Owen couldn't help but wonder how Rowena would compare to her sister, Mildred.

Leo's lips twitched. "She does. As I understand it, Lord Pepperwirth is very protective of Rowena and she's been quite closeted away until now. Say you'll join us and I would be happy to put in a good word for you with her father."

An attendant appeared with a tray, offering two glasses of brandy for Owen and Leo.

"Put mine on my account. I'll pay before I leave tonight," Owen informed the attendant. Once the man had left, they were relatively alone again and Owen faced his friend.

"Does Miss Rowena have any potential suitors who might throw punches too?"

Leo threw back his head in a hearty booming laugh. "Heavens, no. Though she made quite a stir during her presentation. Best if you act fast, woo the young lady before she meets any other men."

Owen sighed. "Very well, I'll come." Wooing was not a problem. He'd been wooing ladies since he was a young man. It was his lack of prospects that damaged his cause. No one wanted to marry a bloody fortune hunter, which was exactly what he was. And he hated it. Chasing women just for money left him hollow but he had no choice. His home, Wesden Heath, was sacred to him. When he'd returned from the war, scarred and broken, the wooded glens and fields of wildflowers had been his healing haven. He couldn't give it up without a fight.

"Excellent. You supping here tonight?" Leo rose from his seat.

"Planned to. You?" Owen rolled his brandy back and forth between his palms before he and Leo exited the gaming room.

"Yes, actually. I'll join you, if you don't mind the company." Leo grinned.

"Only if you tell me more of this young lady I'm to woo." Owen was relieved he and Leo were on good terms again. It wasn't at all the thing to quarrel with one's good friends. Not after everything he'd been through during the war and afterward. Good friends were worth their weight in gold and he would never forsake one, not for anything.

"Well"—Leo glanced about again, apparently determined not to be overheard—"she's quite the beauty, with flaxen hair and cornflower blue eyes..."

~

"WERE YOU NERVOUS, MILLY?"

Mildred Pepperwirth glanced into the mirror of her polished walnut vanity table to meet her younger sister's gaze. They were in a lavish guest room at Hampton House attending a house party through the weekend. It was the first formal dinner party in the country for her sister Rowena to attend since she'd turned eighteen.

"Nervous about what?" Milly waited patiently as their lady's maid Constance tucked the last few tendrils of Milly's chestnut hair into place. The maid had created an elegant coiffure that left a mass of hair in thick, coiled strands almost in a Grecian fashion. A green fade comb studded with diamonds was nestled in the base of her hair, keeping the intricate coils bound together.

Rowena, perched on Milly's bed, was already dressed

in a white lace evening gown, one suitable for a young lady only just come out into society. She tugged on her elbow-length white gloves, fidgeting with them until she'd tugged them too tight and then was forced to loosen them again.

Milly fought off a smile. Her little sister had no reason to be nervous. She was exquisite and every male eye would be on her once she joined the other guests downstairs.

"Oh, you know. The parties, the balls, the suitors?" Rowena's eyes were soft but the same arresting shade of blue that she and Milly had inherited from their father. The brilliant color had captivated many a young man and made many a lady jealous.

"I suppose I was at first," Milly replied. "But it all becomes so tedious." She despised all the social engagements that accompanied a typical season, not because she didn't like dinners and balls or dancing. She loved to dance, loved to visit with friends, but it had only taken her one season to realize that she was nothing more than a broodmare on an auction block. The Season had only one true purpose, she'd come to realize: to secure alliances of the wealthy and elite through marriage. Milly had quickly learned to feign a distaste in dancing to avoid giving the impression she would entertain a man's romantic interest in her.

It wasn't that she didn't want to marry; she was much like any other woman—she longed for a loving husband and a happy marriage like her parents had, but she knew what her parents had was rare. They weren't simply husband and wife. They were partners in everything. From the moment her father had met her mother, they'd known they were meant to be. But Milly hadn't met a single man since her come-out who she felt that instant connection with. She wanted what her parents had. Her mother had an equal say in finances and the control of the house and their investments. Milly wanted that, too, but knew of not one single gentleman of her age who would even consider such an equality in marriage. That meant Milly had no real chance of finding a love match like they had, not one that would give her the freedom she needed.

During her years of private schooling in France, she'd been fortunate to glimpse a freer society for women, but here in England, she was a pawn, a piece to be bargained and bought, based on her family's fortune and her father's lands. The realization was unpleasant and Milly had done the only thing she could think of to avoid marriage to a stranger, or marriage to a man she couldn't stand. She'd become standoffish, mulish even, in the presence of eligible men. If they could not stand her coldness, her feigned arrogance, they left her in peace. It was a lonely peace, though, one without a hope of love. She was not brave like the suffragettes she secretly admired.

She would not have chanced such a strategy to avoid marriage if she didn't know without a doubt her father would never force her to marry. He would let her remain under his care for the rest of his life if she didn't find a man who suited her, which was her plan if she didn't find someone who could give her both freedom and happiness in a marriage. It was a lonely solution, but better than the alternative: forced to live the rest of her life with a man who would never see her full potential as a partner.

If any man viewed her as property to be bought, she could never respect him. Love could not grow in a garden sown with seeds of domestic slavery. The only way she could ever marry would be to find a man who would love her mind, her heart, and her soul and agree that she wasn't a lesser being. He would want to support her when she volunteered to teach children to read, especially girls who could benefit from education and better not only themselves but also their families. Milly needed a man who would stand beside his wife if she attended a suffragette meeting, not one who would ignore her or chastise or even forbid her from supporting her belief in equality between the sexes. But such a man did not exist, at least as far as she could tell.

Rowena got off the bed and came over to stand behind Milly, leaning down a few inches to peer at her own reflection in the mirror. She tweaked the bodice of her gown, tugging it up a little rather than down as most young ladies might.

"I don't think dancing would ever become tedious, but I am so clumsy when I'm nervous. What if I trod on my partner's toes?" Her little sister bit her bottom lip nervously.

"You'll do fine, Rowena. Stay close to me if you get nervous." Milly pinched her cheeks to pinken them a bit before she stood and reached for her black evening gloves.

"I do so love that gown," Rowena sighed.

Milly checked her figure in the full mirror by the dresser. It was a wonderful gown of sapphire blue silk with gold and black netting of lace over the bodice. The netting split apart down the front of her dress below her waist to allow the sapphire paneling to show through as she walked. The train was a little long, but the slight bustle at the back displayed her figure to its best advantage.

Constance shared a little smile with Milly as they both caught Rowena smoothing a hand over her hair before she faced them.

"How do I look?" She performed a little pirouette, her eyes shining with excitement and youth.

"You look splendid, as always." Milly clasped her little sister's hands, glad that with her sister she could be herself, if only a few minutes longer.

"Shall we go down to dinner?" she asked.

"Yes." Rowena raised her chin, a self-confidant smile replacing the girlish eagerness as though she'd become a different woman in an instant.

They departed her room, which lay in the east wing of Hampton House, where most of the guests were staying for the dinner party. A group of gentlemen and a few ladies were waiting at the bottom of the grand staircase for the other guests to come down. All eyes turned to Milly and Rowena as they came into view. Milly paused, letting Rowena have her moment to collect the admiration of the room.

Enjoy it, little sister. Someday you will have to choose your path—wife or spinster. Until she did, Rowena could enjoy her first dinner party. Milly glanced at the faces below and froze. There was one man down there she had no intention of interacting with unless forced. He hadn't been on the formal guest list but had to have been a last-minute addition. His presence wouldn't have stopped her from coming, but lord she so hated to be around men like him...After the last house party at Hampton House, she'd been determined to avoid him if possible.

Mr. Owen Hadley was a fortune hunter. A man like that was dangerous. They cared little or not at all for the women they seduced in an attempt to find suitable heiresses. She stared hard at the man's face for a moment longer, wishing she could will him to disappear. But he stayed right where he was, his presence mocking her for her inability to make him vanish.

His scandalous reputation preceded him, and he left a trail of broken hearts and unmarried ladies who lacked the wealth it was rumored he was seeking behind him. She'd heard far too much about Hadley's history with women. How he'd worked his way into many beds, but the widowed ladies knew better than to marry him. A rich widow had the world at her fingertips, and very rarely did those ladies remarry, because it meant turning over their freedom and money to their new husbands. Milly had to applaud those widows for turning the fortune hunter away. Mr. Hadley was a temptation to sin for any woman.

Even Milly had to admit that as he stood there in his evening suit, dark hair long enough to look a tad too roguish to be fashionable, and that grin that melted a woman's resistance, he looked good. He was tall, *too tall*, but perfect for her, not that she liked that—she *didn't*, of course. She preferred to be an equal height to men, and given that she possessed a little more height than many young ladies, most men of her acquaintance weren't taller than her. Hadley, however, was too tall, almost a head above Milly. It made her feel...vulnerable.

Hadley laughed at something the Earl of Hampton said and then glanced up the stairs. His eyes flicked over her briefly, a hint of a frown touching his sensual lips; then his focus turned to Rowena and damn him, the man's hazel eyes lit up with a piercing fire.

Milly's stomach clenched and she froze on the stairs, one gloved hand clasped to her breast.

Rowena. Not her sweet Rowena. The man could seduce any lady, but not her little sister. Rowena needed a good match. Scandal would ruin her beyond redemption and she would be forced out of polite society.

I will have to distract him, even if it will be most distasteful.

Squaring her shoulders, Milly walked down the last two steps and greeted her hosts. The Dowager Countess of Hampton; her soon-to-be-husband, Mr. Leighton; and his daughter, Ivy, along with Leo Graham, the Earl of Hampton.

"You look splendid," Ivy said as she took Milly's arm.

Milly never failed to be surprised at Ivy Leighton's friendliness. The young woman was half Gypsy by her father, and her mother had been a lady's maid. It was in every instinct Milly possessed to treat Ivy coolly given her status as nouveau riche, which happened to be below Milly's own long-generation titled lineage. The first time they'd been introduced, Milly had certainly acted unpleasant. She regretted that. *Immensely*. Her frustration with Leo's intent to propose to her had put a damper on her mood. Milly had been so focused on convincing the earl that she wasn't a good match for him that she'd acted rather callously and arrogantly with regard to everyone around her. Ivy had been a victim of her behavior, and in the last few weeks Milly had made every effort to be deserving of the friendship that Ivy offered.

Ivy had been persistent, and Milly had found herself unable to dislike the young woman once they'd spent a few afternoon teas together discussing literature and politics. They had much in common in their views with regard to women and the rights they unfairly lacked in society.

Milly tilted her head close to Ivy to whisper, "What is Mr. Hadley doing here? As I understood it, he and Lord Hampton had a falling out at the last house party." It had been quite a scandal. Mr. Hadley had left during the middle of a shooting party with a black eye and a sour temper.

Milly allowed Ivy to guide her away from the other guests into an alcove where they could have a small amount of privacy. Ivy's bright caramel eyes darkened a little.

"I'm not sure, but Leo insists they are still friends and that Mr. Hadley no longer has intentions of trying to steal me from Leo."

Milly huffed in reply. "Of course he doesn't, because he's eyeing my sister like a fine glass of sherry he wants to taste." She glowered at the accused seducer, hoping that he could feel the sting of her gaze. He turned and raised one brow in challenge at her from across the room.

"Milly," Ivy gasped, but it soon turned to a giggle as she followed Milly's fixed attention.

"He does look a little too interested. It's a good thing the seating arrangement at dinner keeps him away from Rowena."

Milly touched her throat as she readjusted the diamond necklace that lay against her collarbone. "Who's the unfortunate party guest that must endure his conversation?"

Ivy shot her a sideways glance. "Why you, Milly dear."

For a moment, Milly simply couldn't process what her friend had just told her. She'd been resolved to distract him from Rowena but that didn't include seating next to the odious man at dinner.

"Absolutely no—" Milly was silenced as the butler announced dinner was prepared. "Ivy, I'm not sitting next to that man," she hissed in her friend's ear.

Ivy merely laughed. "Someone has to and who better than you? I think you're a perfect match in ill tempers." The teasing comment made Milly frown deeply. Even though she'd been seemingly ill-tempered on purpose, it wasn't who she really was. Deep down, she was a woman who wanted love and laughter in her life. But a man like Hadley would never see the real her, nor would a man like him want a real partner in life. He only wanted a wife for money. He embodied everything she hated.

Chapter Two

The ladies went from the drawing room to the lavish dining room first. Milly blanched as she went to her seat. A footman stepped out of the shadows, pulled her chair back, and seated her. She felt like a man doomed to die by hanging, waiting on the scaffold for the quick drop and the final stop. She had to deal with Mr. Hadley. There was something unsettling about being too close to him, the scent of sandalwood and pine that she caught as she stood only a few feet away from him, and the way his lips curved up in a wry smile as she came closer. It made her knees buckle and her pulse pound. Nothing about Mr. Hadley made her feel stable and in control.

Still, it was better that she do it than Rowena. Her younger sister might fall for the dark-haired seducer with his devilish smiles and hearty laughter. Yes, it was a good thing Rowena was seated closer to the quiet and handsome Scottish Earl of Forres. He was a much safer dinner companion than a fortune hunter like Hadley.

"Miss Pepperwirth," Mr. Hadley greeted coldly as he took a seat beside her once all the ladies and remaining gentlemen had taken their seats.

"Good evening, Mr. Hadley," she replied just as coolly. By the end of the third course, they'd likely frost their end of the table over with their chilled politeness.

"Are you enjoying the weather?" His question surprised her, and she answered before thinking through her response.

"The weather? It is October, Mr. Hadley, a lovely autumnal month. Of course I enjoy it." She hadn't meant to say that, hadn't meant to reveal anything about herself that she enjoyed. It made her likeable, and that meant suitors would notice her. She couldn't allow that.

"You enjoy October, then? What about it do you like?" He dipped his spoon into his bowl of cream of watercress soup and then after tasting it, angled his body toward her. It was inappropriate to do so, but no one else seemed to notice his position or his focus on her.

His eyes met hers and she saw a challenging gleam in his gaze underlaid with other more confusing emotions... heat, but not anger. She met him stare for stare despite the fact that his gaze made her feel as naked as though she wore nothing more than a corset and chemise.

A sudden flush heated Milly's body from the tips of her toes to her cheeks. How could a simple move, his body turned toward her in a close setting, make her react so...strongly?

Like a fever. The thought only just penetrated the haze that lingered at the edge of her mind and body. She brought herself out of it with a little shake of her head.

"I'm sorry, what did you ask me?" For the life of her she couldn't remember his question.

"October, what do you like about it?" He was blatantly ignoring the woman on his right and a few people across the table were noticing.

Milly swallowed hard and reached for her water goblet. Her tongue felt a little thick and her throat dry. Hadley's intense focus on her was unsettling.

"I...uh...enjoy the changing of the colors of the leaves, the way the crisp breeze has a slight bite to it."

Oh dear, I'm rambling. She hastily took a few sips of her watercress soup, not daring to look in Hadley's direction. When he said nothing, she finally was forced to look his way. Those eyes, the ones that promised danger and seduction, were entirely fixed on her. How could he make her feel so naked and excited? As though she had no secrets from him and with that glint of arrogance she saw, he knew *exactly* what she was thinking. She stared back at him, her heart thumping hard enough that she wondered if her ribs would be bruised on the morrow.

"And you, Mr. Hadley. What do you like about October?"

He chuckled. "I don't like the month. Not at all. I prefer June or July. The heat, you know, I like that much better. The feel of the sun warming my bare skin...a man can grow addicted to the feel of that pleasurable burning, perhaps even a woman can, too."

The heat? He liked the heat? She very much doubted that he meant the heat of the sun. No, she sensed that the heat he referred to was something else entirely, something she wasn't supposed to know about, being a virgin, and yet she did. She only knew enough to know it was bad to think of words like *heat* and *pleasurable burning* in such a scandalous fashion. There was something about the way he said the words and how his eyes darkened as he looked at her that made it feel so wrong. So wrong in a delicious way like eating the last bit of dessert when she'd already had too much.

"You don't like the heat?" Owen finally broke his stare and turned to face his bowl of soup again.

With his concentration on her disrupted, Milly's strength returned. "No. I most certainly do not."

With a practiced ease, Mr. Hadley tossed one shoulder in a casual shrug and replied,

"Pity, it might have been fun for you and I to enjoy the summer heat together." And then he didn't converse with her for the remainder of the dinner.

For some reason, it made her angry, angry and a little hurt. Which made no sense, since she didn't like him. Despised him, in fact. Then why did it sting? She shouldn't want him to continue talking to her or discussing things that were likely far too scandalous for dinner, but there had been something to him when he spoke to her. She'd felt...alive even as they'd played whatever sort of game he'd started and she missed the feeling of excitement that came with verbally sparring with him, even for so short a time.

For the remainder of the meal, she partook minimally in the other conversations, still mulling over Owen's words and what they really meant...and more importantly how his heated gaze had made her feel.

After dinner, Milly spent the remainder of the evening, while the men were unaware, speaking with Ivy about joining the local suffragettes for their meetings. If Milly was to remain unwed, she wanted to devote her life to her passion—the education of women—and Ivy had some wonderful ideas of how Milly could become involved. It left her feeling full of hope for the first time in years. She would have a purpose, one not buried by society's expectations but rather one that would challenge her and give young girls a sense of a future that was bright and filled with chances they would never have dreamed of without proper education.

It was a long while later when the ladies were finally

ready to go to bed. The gentlemen had gone to drink port in another part of the large manor house and the ladies of the party were thankfully in agreement that it was time to retire.

Milly joined Rowena as they ascended the main set of stairs and walked down the hall to their wing. Their rooms were opposite each other in the hall.

"Rowena, remember to lock your door after Constance sees to you," she reminded her little sister.

"My door...why of course, but why would you tell me to?" Rowena entered her chamber, where Constance stood waiting. Pinching her earrings off and her delicate diamond bracelets, she handed them to their maid, who carried them over to a sateen jewelry box on the dresser.

"It's Mr. Hadley. I don't like the way he was looking at you tonight." Milly leaned against one of the bedposts, gripping the wood between her gloved hands.

"How was he looking at me? What do you mean, Milly?" Her little sister's eyes were wide and a little fearful.

"You're too young to know what sort of man he is, but trust me when I say you don't want to be someone he is interested in. Fortune hunters are heartless. They only care about the money they can get when they ruin you. I saw the way he was looking at you tonight. I believe he might try to seduce you. You could not survive the scandal if he did. You must take care not to be anywhere alone, especially with him. After dinner tonight, I was worried he might try to visit your rooms. It is the easiest way to compromise a woman."

At this her sister froze, her gown half undone in the back. Constance even paused in the act of slipping buttons of their slits.

"He'll try to compromise me?"

Milly sighed. Her sister was so innocent, like a sacrificial lamb.

"Yes. He'd compromise you. Come to your chambers in nothing but a dressing gown, climb into your bed, and arrange to be discovered with you." Milly paused. She wasn't all that sure of what followed except there might be a fair amount of kissing and something about a man lying atop a woman.

"Oh, Milly, you mean you think he'd..." Rowena made a funny little gesture with her hands by squishing them together almost as if she were in prayer.

Milly nodded. "He would force himself on you."

Rowena gasped.

It was a fate worse than death in Milly's eyes. Being compromised and then forced to marry the man who ruined you. Men who did that to women didn't love them, and a marriage without love was something she never wanted to contemplate.

"My lady." Constance flashed Milly a panicked look because Rowena had turned a frightening ashen white.

Milly grasped her sister by the shoulders, giving her a gentle shake.

"Rowena, I'm so sorry. I didn't mean to frighten you. I'm sure Mr. Hadley wouldn't hurt you. He seems only to break hearts, not other things. I do not believe he'd do any real harm, except to your reputation. But you must take care all the same. Lock your door."

When her sister nodded, her eyes still as round as teacup saucers, Milly kissed her cheek and then left to cross the hall to her own room to prepare for bed. She unfastened her necklace and removed her earrings before she slid her black gloves off and laid them down over the back of a chair. She would have to wait for Constance to assist her, so she seated herself at the vanity table. What a night she'd had, suffering Mr. Hadley's strange behavior at dinner. Had he meant to tease her the way a cat did a mouse? It seemed likely he'd only attempted conversation with her out of boredom.

A pity that, she thought. *I would have loved to have a genuine conversation with anyone, even him.* But all the things she longed to discuss, like politics or history, were not favorable topics for a lady to discuss. In France, she'd been able to speak so freely to men about her opinions. Back in England she'd been forced to accept the fact that the life she'd been living in France would likely never be possible here. Men still wished to go to separate rooms to smoke, leaving women to their idle gossip. She knew Ivy and Leo broke from tradition frequently and would sit and talk for hours about things that *mattered*.

I wish I could have that. The longing for it was so desperate that it left her feeling empty and cold because she feared she would never find a man who would wish to do that with her.

For a moment, she thought of Owen's flashing dark eyes and the way he'd riled her temper up as they'd talked but how he'd also made her feel things she hadn't ever felt before.

Heat. The word he'd used to tease her seemed to make her entire body burn at the thought. If she had to be completely honest with herself, his teasing had been enjoyable. But admitting that made her frown. He was a fortune hunter and she shouldn't enjoy his attentions. Of course, she had no reason to worry; he had no real interest in her.

Men like him, while they loved the challenge of seducing women, wouldn't be overly interested in someone like her, not when easy prey like her little sister was available. Envy slithered beneath her skin in that moment and she wished, at least some small part of her did, that Owen wanted her, not Rowena. It was foolish, nonsensical, but part of her longed to be desired. But it didn't matter; she was in no danger of ever being married at this rate, nor would she ever be the subject of a fortune hunter's seductions. She'd developed her prickly exterior too well to stop even the most determined man from trying to woo her. But that didn't stop her from wanting the right man, the one who would love her, to see through her façade.

Milly was still brooding when Constance entered her bedchamber and came over to help her undress. After the layers of silk dropped to the floor and her corset and chemise were removed, Constance held out a long, comfortable, elegant nightdress with fine lace trimmed with ribbon inserts. Milly tugged her hair into a loose rope to one side and plucked a blue ribbon from her jewelry case and tied it in a bow around her hair at the nape of her neck.

"Ready for bed, milady?" Constance asked as she turned down Milly's bed.

"Yes," she replied, extremely weary.

She'd been up since dawn, helping Rowena prepare for the social niceties that would occur tonight and on future nights during her first Season. Rowena had been understandably concerned that she would make a mistake tonight. She hadn't, of course; she had behaved beautifully. Milly could not have been prouder of her. The handsome Earl of Forres, who'd traveled all the way from Scotland for this house party, had even shown an interest in Rowena. According to Ivy, Forres was recently widowed and the father of a beautiful two-year-old daughter he'd brought down to England. He and his daughter had stayed here for a few weeks with the Dowager Countess of Hampton, who was some distant relation of his.

"I'll come check on you in the morning when I bring your tea and scones." Constance smiled and took her leave.

Milly climbed onto the bed and pulled the bedclothes up around her chest and sighed. The bed was so large, and rather lonely. Usually she didn't let such a melancholy thought bother her, but tonight for some reason, it did. There was a dull ache in her chest and she rubbed the spot with her hand. Somewhere tonight, Mr. Hadley was likely climbing into bed, dreaming of all the young ladies' hearts he would steal and break. A treacherous little flutter in her chest made Milly wince. She ought not to think of Hadley, certainly not while she was in bed...yet thinking of him, as frustrating and maddeningly irritating as he was, flushed her with a welcome heat in the chilly room.

The oil lamp beside her bed was the only light left in the room and it burned steadily. Often she read late into the night and forgot to turn it off, but tonight she was too tired to read. She reached over and gently twisted the brass knob to kill the little flame. Darkness absorbed the dying light and Milly flipped onto her back. The cold of the sheets almost stung her bare toes and legs when her night-dress rode up to her knees. A cold bed, an empty bed. It shouldn't have upset her, but after Mr. Hadley's talk of heat and summer, she was off balance and bothered.

The mere thought of him and the way his eyes had darkened and seemed to shimmer with inner flames brought on another rush of warmth. His eyes, like honeyed fire, and his lips, the way he'd smiled sardonically, almost mockingly, in a way she rather liked, irritated her, yet fascinated her. There was no reason to like a man's mouth or to imagine what it might be like to have that mouth pressed to hers in a kiss that caused the heat he was so fond of discussing. She knew his kiss would be hot, because when she thought of it, her body blossomed with a swelling of heat in her belly. *His mouth is wicked... sinful...and I hate that I wish to know how he tastes.* It was a forbidden thought, but one she couldn't deny. She rolled over onto her stomach, fluffed her pillow, and squeezed her eyes shut, attempting to will herself to sleep. It was going to be a long night.

Chapter Three

Owen paced the length of his bedchamber, wearing light trousers and a dressing gown, but no shirt. His valet, Evans, had come and gone, having helped him undress and put away neckcloths, cuff links, and a hundred other minor details of Owen's wardrobe. Normally he and Evans would converse at length on any number of topics but tonight he had one thing on his mind.

Rowena Pepperwirth.

Such a lovely young lady and perfect for his needs. Even though he hadn't had a chance to speak with her that evening, he'd seen enough to know he'd happily bed her. He'd asked Evans tonight to discern where his future bride was sleeping. Apparently, she was in the opposite wing, just past the suit of armor on the left.

Owen checked the clock on the marble mantelpiece above the fireplace in his chamber. Half-past midnight. Surely she was asleep by now. All he needed to do was slip inside her chamber and wait to be "discovered" when Evans found a reason to have Rowena's mother come to check on her. Stalking over to the door, he cracked it open and peered into the hall. Empty. No servants were within sight and no houseguests either.

He slipped out of his bedroom and hastily took the route Evans had described. The golden light of the hall lamps and the rich red carpet made the hall feel warm and cheery. It put him in good spirts. This plan was going to work. He paused at reaching the chain-mail knight. His reflection in the shiny helmet was almost comical and he smiled. After tonight his future would be secured; he would have a lovely young bride and Wesden Heath would have a fortune to sustain it. He just hated that he had to secure his home by such dastardly means. He'd tried wooing widows and heiresses the last year with no success. Desperation had driven him to this foolish scheme but he couldn't turn back.

Two more steps and he was facing Rowena's door: the woman who would become his wife, albeit through scandalous measures. But Wesden Heath needed to be protected and supported.

"You've got this, old boy," he muttered in encourage-

ment, and reached for the door handle. The latch clicked down and the door pushed inward to the darkened room.

Good. She was asleep. Padding softly into the room, he closed the door behind him. It was impossible to see except for the sliver of light cutting through the thick baize curtains in front of the window. Eventually his eyes adjusted to the lack of light and he made out a bed against one wall. Walking carefully over to the window, he swept a hand between the curtains, pushing them apart. Milky moonlight now bathed the bed and its occupant enough to tease Owen with a view of a languidly stretched body with healthy curves. Bedding Rowena once they were married would be a most enjoyable experience, and he would teach the innocent young lady how to seek her own pleasure, too. He wanted his marriage bed to be full of mutual desire and ecstasy. A woman who was well loved in bed made a happy woman out of bed. And he planned to see to his future wife's happiness once they'd settled in at Wesden Heath.

Rowena shifted in the bed, sighed, and kicked one leg free of her blankets. Silky white skin made his fingers ache to stroke up from her delicate ankle to her upper thigh. Lord, the temptation to touch her, to take what he wanted, was so strong, but he mastered his control. Rowena suddenly rolled restlessly in his direction and then she gasped.

"Who are you?" Her voice was a panicked whisper.

"It is me, Owen, Hadley. I've come to—"

"Mr. Hadley?" The outrage in her tone was surprisingly forceful and her voice was deeper than he remembered, a sensual huskiness of a grown woman, rather than a young woman of eighteen.

"Rowena." He paused, unsure of what to say, but she sat bolt upright in bed and fumbled with the wooden nightstand. A rasp of a match and then an oil lamp bloomed, casting a light on the woman in his bed.

"Good God," he cursed.

Mildred, not Rowena, glowered at him, her long dark chestnut hair in a luscious tangle of wild waves about her shoulders. For a moment, he was utterly distracted by the thought of threading his fingers through her hair as he tilted her head back for a kiss.

"Mr. Hadley, leave my chamber at once before someone sees you." Mildred only then seemed to realize her nightdress had ridden up her legs and she tugged it down before she slid out of bed. The fabric clung to her more than she expected it to.

"Please, Mr. Hadley."

Her plea broke through the haze of his building curiosity and desire.

Right, Mildred, must leave now...Sanity restored itself in rapid fire and he headed for the door. The moment his hand touched the knob, he had to stumble back as it opened. A lady's maid with a shawl about her shoulders and a lamp in one hand froze upon seeing him.

"My lady...," the woman murmured in a hushed sound of shock.

The situation was far worse than Owen could have predicted. Lady Pepperwirth in her dressing gown and hair unbound, stood just behind the maid, her keen eyes sweeping over Owen and the scene with surprise.

"Constance said she was informed you'd taken ill, Milly dear," Lady Pepperwirth said, but her frown said everything her words did not. "It seems it is not an illness that plagues you, but something else."

"Mama, Mr. Hadley came here by mistake. He was just leaving—"

Lady Pepperwirth entered the room and motioned for Constance to come in as well.

"Silence, Milly. The damage is done. The four of us know what has happened tonight, but we cannot let word spread or else we will have a serious problem." Lady Pepperwirth turned on Owen. "You, Mr. Hadley, will ask for Milly's hand tomorrow by speaking with my husband. I will tell him he should accept and the wedding will be done within a few weeks. If anyone asks, you two have had a secret understanding the last year and are now to be married. Is that understood?"

Owen sputtered. "I..."

"You'll be properly compensated, Mr. Hadley. My eldest daughter's dowry is far larger than Rowena's is."

Could the viscountess read his mind?

"That is what you were concerned about, was it not?" Lady Pepperwirth's chilly stare almost made him flinch.

Owen cleared his throat and nodded. "I will be honored to ask for Miss Pepperwirth's hand first thing tomorrow."

"Good. Now, I suggest we all retire for the night. Many preparations will need to be made on the morrow." Lady Pepperwirth opened the door and nudged a still-stunned Constance out into the hallway.

For a long moment, Owen couldn't move. His mind was blank and he felt as though his feet were rooted to the carpet.

"What have you done?" Mildred hissed.

Her chiding tone got under his skin and he spun to face her.

"I've gotten us engaged, that's what I've done, and we cannot get out of it." He shoved his hands into his robe's pockets, fuming.

Mildred walked right up to him and jabbed a finger into his bare chest through the parted robe.

"You thought I was Rowena. It was her you meant to compromise, wasn't it?"

He grasped her wrist, but rather than push her hand away, he held on to it, admiring the soft, warm skin beneath his hand. Her pulse raced wildly at that delicate point on her inner wrist where his fingers curled around it.

I should let go. But he didn't. He was staring at her bright blue eyes so full of fire and those soft rosebud lips in a pout that made him want to kiss them, perhaps take a nibble...

"Hadley, are you listening to me?" She struggled to free her wrist from his hand.

"Mildred, please, call me Owen. We are to be married." He tried to bite back a sudden smile at the entire ridiculous situation. Neither of them had wanted this, and he felt damned awful for upsetting Mildred. It was clear she didn't want to be married and while he didn't exactly like her, at least in the traditional sense, he didn't want to upset her. The honest truth was he had destroyed both their lives, but more so hers than his. He'd been ready to marry a stranger—and it was clear Mildred was not—and he hated causing her the pain that he saw in her eyes despite her rising ire.

He wasn't sure if it was a nightmare to be married to her or not. He would have to wait and find out. There was something undeniably fascinating about riling Mildred's temper. Even if he was condemned to marry the harpy, he could at least laugh about it.

"Fine. Owen. And if you call me Mildred again, I'll..."

His lips twitched. "You prefer Milly, then? So do I. Thank heavens we agree on one thing at least."

Her feminine huff of displeasure made him chuckle. Just like October and July. They were opposites. What a dreadful match they would make. Yet, since he was doomed, he might as well embrace the absurdity of knowing he would be marrying her in a few weeks.

"You've ruined everything!" Milly snapped, but he saw the glimmer of hurt in her eyes rather than anger. Had she loved another? Was he robbing her of a man she'd intended to marry?

"Milly, did you..." He swallowed before continuing. "Did you have an understanding with another man?" Why he wanted her to say no he wasn't sure. The thought of her weeping into a pillow over someone else after she became his was not a pleasant thought, not that he wanted her. He didn't. He wanted Rowena.

Milly sighed, a little tear dripping down her right cheek as she pulled her wrist free of his grasp. She walked around him to her bed and sat on the edge, tucking her knees up under her chin like a child.

"I didn't want to marry anyone, not like this..." She sniffed and looked up at him. "And now I'm to be stuck with you." She waved a hand at him and then sniffed again, her eyes too bright, too full of tears. Had he ever believed Milly Pepperwirth capable of crying? No, he hadn't. She'd always been this bastion of female spinsterdom to him. Beautiful, but cold and untouchable. Who was this teary-eyed beauty who lit an unwelcome yet undeniable fire in his blood?

He was moving before he was aware of it. He eased down beside her on the bed and cupped her chin, turning her face toward his.

"Milly, I'm sorry I've done this to you, to both of us." He meant it. They were stuck with each other and it was his fault. She didn't deserve this fate and he was a coward for compromising her like this and forcing her into it. The hard lump in his throat made it hard to breathe for a moment.

Her long lashes fluttered, tears coating her lips like tiny crystals. This wasn't the angry woman from dinner earlier that evening; this woman was vulnerable and oddly beautiful despite her eyes reddened with tears. His chest tightened as he faced the fact that he had made her weep. Owen couldn't help but wonder if her aloof act was truly that, *an act*.

"Then don't go see my father tomorrow. Just leave. I'll not tell a soul what happened."

He shook his head. "The damage is done." He shifted a few inches closer, his hand on her chin sliding around to cup her cheek. Her skin was soft as silk and he half closed his eyes as he fixed on her lips. He had the sudden urge to taste her, a woman he couldn't stand.

"Let me kiss you," he begged in a ragged whisper.

Swept away by a surge of desire, he wanted to taste this woman's lips to see how fiery she was when she wasn't verbally sparring with him.

"What?" She blinked in surprise and drew back an inch.

Every predatory instinct in him took over and he dipped his head, brushing his lips over hers, light enough for her to still withdraw or to lean forward. Her mouth trembled against his and he felt her lean in, just a bare quarter inch. He curled his fingers around the back of her neck and held her still for his plundering kiss. He tasted her, teased her lips, and stroked the tip of his tongue along the seam of her mouth. A soft little throaty sound escaped Milly and he wanted to crow in triumph as she kissed him back. The lady could be seduced after all!

It took a surprising amount of willpower for him to separate their mouths. He rested his forehead against hers and stroked her cheeks with his thumbs as they shared panting breaths.

"I know this isn't what you wanted, and I am sorry." He kissed her again, this time on her cheek, and exited the room before she could say another word or shed another tear that he would see.

Chapter Four

Three weeks later. Three *long* weeks later, Milly was standing at the altar of a small church in the village outside of Pepperwirth Vale, her family's home. Owen stood next to her, dressed in his finest morning dress, which should have made the man look respectable but all it did was make him look wicked, in a way that would leave all the ladies in the pews behind her green with envy.

They'd spent the three weeks leading up to this moment in each other's company on an almost daily basis and she was coming to learn that he wasn't as heartless as she thought he was, but it didn't change the fact that she didn't want to be here at the altar facing a life with this man. Even though he did make a fine groom...

Blast it! I don't even want him as my husband. I don't.

Owen glanced her way, one dark brow raised as though he'd heard her wildly inappropriate thoughts.

"It's time for the ring," he whispered loud enough for only her to hear.

A silly blush flushed her cheeks as she held out her gloved hand. They were specially made bridal gloves where the silk on the ring finger could be removed, her ring placed on, and the silk drawn back over it. Owen did all of this methodically, but a second before he slid the band on her finger, his hand shook and he nearly dropped it. As the band settled against her skin and he gingerly slid the silk fingerlet back on, they shared a sigh of relief, and for one single instant they shared a smile, too, a small, fatigued one, but shared nonetheless. Strangely, in that moment, she didn't feel alone. They were both facing this life together.

The remainder of the ceremony was a blur. Milly had Rowena and Ivy as her bridesmaids and they took great care to arrange her long cream silk train as she was prepared to walk down the aisle. Owen waited patiently, his forearm held out toward her. She glanced at it, then up at him. He gave her the barest hint of a nod in encouragement. The last thing she wanted was to touch him—she was still furious with him—but she felt a little lightheaded and her tulle veil seemed to weigh heavily on her head. Having something solid to grip would help.

Her fingers curled around his arm, clinging to the fabric of his sleeve.

"Ready?" he asked.

"Yes, please just do not let me trip," she begged him. The voluminous skirts of her lovely gown were far more fabric than she was used to, and given how frantic her heart was beating made her feel unsteady on her feet.

"I've got you." Owen's body was warm and hard beside her own, which was an unexpected but welcomed comfort. He covered her hand on his arm with his free hand, patting it gently.

At least in this we are united, she thought.

They walked down the aisle together, stepping over a trail of rose petals as they headed to the entrance of the church. There would be a light meal taken by her family and Owen before they would leave for his estate. Wesden Heath. She knew so little of the man she'd married. Her husband. How strange the word felt on her tongue. All she knew was that his lands were nestled somewhere in the small region of the Cotswolds.

During their time together in the last three weeks leading up to the wedding, he had spoken of his home fondly, the soft smile on his full lips lighting up his eyes. She'd felt melancholy to think she would leave Pepperwirth Vale because she felt the same way about her own home as he did his. But she had to go with him now; as his wife, she could not stay here with her parents and hide away any longer. New fears had replaced her old ones. What was to come? Would he abandon her at the estate and return to London to conduct affairs with mistresses?

Milly flinched, trying not to think of that. First, she had to survive her wedding night. Owen had mentioned the day before they would take a coach to an inn halfway to his estate. Milly knew she couldn't protest any of his plans, but a tiny part of her was frightened at leaving Pepperwirth Vale permanently. It was one thing to travel and come back, but Pepperwirth Vale would no longer be her home after tonight. Perhaps it was usual for some women to be fine with abandoning their homes when they married, but she was a woman who grew roots where she lived and felt connected to the place where she made a life for herself. Wesden Heath would have to be her new home and she would have to learn to grow comfortable there.

"Milly, what's the matter?" Owen had stopped them in front of their coach, which would take them back to her parents' home for them to dine and change.

"Hmm?" she replied, glancing about at the wedding attendees who were filing out of their church after them, laughing and smiling. A few already threw rice at them.

"You have a viselike grip on my arm," Owen said, looking more than a little concerned, given the way his brows drew together.

Forcing herself to unfist her fingers, she dropped her hand from his arm and sighed. "I'm sorry."

"It's all right, Milly. No need to apologize." He helped Ivy and Rowena gather her skirts and then caught her by the waist and lifted her into the carriage.

When they were both seated, alone except for the driver in the front, she turned to Owen.

"You can stop that, you know." She set her bouquet on the seat across from them and glowered. Between the kiss he'd given her on the night they were discovered and the gentle, caring façade he was showing now, she wanted to scream. No woman liked knowing a man was placating her. If she was to be trapped, he shouldn't condescend to treat her like a skittish horse.

"Stop what?" Owen tugged on the edges of his gloves and curled his fingers to better the fit of the gloves.

"Treating me so nicely. You don't have to pretend. Our situation is bad enough. We ought not to add lies or false behavior to this farce."

The horrid man laughed. "You have a sharp tongue, wife. I had hoped marriage would tame that shrewish temper." He leaned back in the open carriage, striking a pose of a man so at ease that Milly snapped.

"You cad!" She retrieved her bouquet from the opposite seat and leaned over to smack him in the chest with the flowers. Petals exploded in a floral burst and the light breeze from the carriage's forward movement caught the petals and scattered them all over the interior of the coach and on their clothes. The people standing on the church steps burst into laughter at the sight of the wind and the flowers dancing around them.

"What the devil?" Owen bolted upright, trying to brush the flowers off his lap, and he fixed Milly with a narrowed gaze. "I'm not opposed to putting you over my knee!" The sharpness of his eyes lit with a heat that startled her. The threat seemed more sensual, as though he didn't plan to harm her. For some reason that infuriated her all the more.

"Put me over your knee?" Her voice was shrill, even to her own ears. "How like a man! And you wondered why I never wanted to marry?" She slapped a palm to his chest, attempting to shove him away, but he curled an arm around her waist and dragged her across his lap. She was still sputtering in outrage when he slanted his mouth over hers. This was no sweet, lingering brush of lips like that night in her room. It was hot, wet, delicious, and wicked. Her lower belly quivered and her hands flattened on his chest before curling into fists as she relaxed. It was impossible not to enjoy this.

His hand cupped her cheek and he whispered against her lips, "Open your mouth."

"Open my—" Her confusion was replaced with shock when he took advantage of her parted lips and slid his tongue inside. The odd sensation, the eroticism of it, was too much. Milly squirmed as part of her lower body throbbed to life, almost hurting with an intense ache. How could Owen of all men affect her like this? She didn't like him.

What's wrong with me? Was a woman supposed to feel such things for a man? She'd heard the occasional rumor, but that's what she believed it was. Rumor and nothing more...but this...this was not fantasy. This was hard, sharp, wonderfully confusing, pleasurable reality.

"There now." Owen stroked a fingertip across her bottom lip. "Feeling less shrewish?" The devilish glint in his eye said he was teasing, but it still upset her. She didn't want a man to call her a shrew, especially not her husband. It hurt. She wasn't shrewish; she just hated being forced to marry a man she was quite certain would never see her as more than a bank account.

"You used my body against me!" she accused, fully aware she was still in his lap, clinging to his coat like a startled kitten, but she couldn't seem to let go of him.

"You know," he said thoughtfully, "I'll wager that if you stopped fighting yourself, you might be happier with our situation."

"Happy being married to you? Not until pigs have wings!" She finally had the good sense to scramble off his lap, and he let her. A tiny part of her, just a sliver, was disappointed he didn't fight to keep her close.

I should be grateful, not disappointed. But there was no

denying the presence of that traitorous emotion. She buried it deep inside her and focused on the light meal they would have at her home and the long travel ahead with her husband.

What am I going to do? Alone with him for the rest of my life...He will never want me, never see me as an equal in our marriage. He wasn't like her papa and wouldn't value her the way her father did her mother. She'd be alone, just as she'd vowed she'd always wanted, even if it felt like such an awful lie. Why did it now seem such an unbearable fate?

OWEN TOOK A STRANGE PLEASURE IN LIFTING Milly down from the carriage. Her cheeks were still a pretty pink, like alabaster touched with rose. He had enjoyed silencing her with a kiss and relished her startled response. And she had responded, quite well. His shrewish wife had a soft, sensual side that, he had to admit, fascinated him.

The previous evening he had listened to her converse with the other guests during a dinner party prior to the wedding day and found she had a sharp mind. There was more to her than he'd expected. Most daughters of the peerage went away for school and came back educated, but they often reminded him of the parrots he'd seen while fighting in the war in Africa. They could repeat fancy phrases that had been told to them but had no original thoughts.

That wasn't the case with Milly. She had opinions, well-formed ones, and he rather liked knowing that his wife wouldn't be some foolish creature obsessed with gossip and the latest Parisian fashions. Not that Milly didn't look exceedingly fine and had excellent taste in clothes. He'd be the first to admit she was stunning. When she'd entered the church that morning, he'd forgotten to breathe, and only when she'd gotten closer to him, he'd realized his lungs were burning and he'd sucked in a breath. He wanted to laugh at himself, and at this entire situation. He'd ended up with the most beautiful wife a man could hope for, one with a quick wit and intelligence and lips made for kissing, and yet she despised him. That bothered him more than it should have; even though he was seeking a bride for monetary gain, he had hoped whoever he ended up marrying would in fact enjoy being with him, both in bed and out.

Owen glanced at her as their carriage rolled up in front of Pepperwirth Vale. Her cheeks were still flushed from their kiss, even though it had been a quarter of an hour since they'd left the church. Yes, she despised him, but when they'd been locked in that embrace, he'd tasted her passion, her longing, her desire. The question was, could he turn that into something more?

I bloody well hope so...

When he set her down on the gravel drive just a few feet from the door, a row of servants watched them placidly as they waited to assist. Two upstairs maids rushed over to catch the expensive silk train of the gown and carry it inside behind Milly as she walked.

She looked brilliant, parading regally through the door of her ancestral home, her chin in the air. Her beautiful chestnut hair was caught in a loose coiling of curls and knots, with diamond star hairpins holding the folded veil in place. When she paused at the bottom stair of the main staircase, one elegant gloved hand on the rail, her figure with perfect curves, meant for a man's hands, was presented in a queenly pose. Again, Owen had to remind himself to breathe. She was a picture of radiance and she was *his*.

"I'm sure, Mr. Aslet, our butler, has a room prepared for you to change into your traveling clothes."

"Er...yes, thank you," he mumbled, still a little distracted as he watched his bride ascend the stairs. The way the light slanted in from the windows on either side made her dress and the large bow above her delectable bottom seem to glow with a heavily light, which only tempted him more.

"Mr. Hadley, I'll show you to your room, if you're ready." Mr. Aslet was a tall, thin man, his body all sharp angles and precision.

Owen nodded and followed Aslet up the stairs and down a hall in the opposite direction Milly had gone.

His travel trunk was sitting on the bed, the items for his upcoming journey laid out. Trousers, a coat, and boots. He'd sent his valet Evans and Milly's maid, Constance, ahead to Wesden Heath, where he and Milly would meet with the servants on the morrow. Milly had assured him that she could make do one night without a maid. Owen doubted that, but he thought it would be amusing to see her try. He stripped out of his morning clothes and tucked them into his trunk and then dressed in his travel clothes before he came back down the stairs. Two footmen were bringing trays into the dining room. He started toward the room, but before he could reach it, Rowena and Milly's parents came in through the entrance.

"Ahh, Mr. Hadley, if you don't mind, could we have a word in my study?" Lord Pepperwirth waved a hand to show the way.

"Of course." He followed Milly's father, reluctant to know what the man had to say. Lord Pepperwirth had done a fine job raking him over the coals the morning following his discovery in Milly's bedchamber. But after the harsh dressing down for his behavior, the man had seemed a little amused that he'd finally arranged a match for Milly.

When they entered Lord Pepperwirth's study, he

beckoned for Owen to sit in one of the plush leather chairs facing the large Chippendale desk. Lord Pepperwirth sat down and stroked one hand over his dark beard that was streaked with silver.

"Milly is...difficult sometimes," he began.

Owen held his breath for a second, wondering where this conversation was going to lead.

"But she's incredibly bright, like her mother. She's the sort of woman that if given half the chance, can be an asset to a man's life, not a hindrance." His blue eyes, so much like his two daughters', pinned Owen to his chair.

"I consented to this ludicrous wedding because my wife insisted it was the only way to save Milly's reputation. I know it may be in a man's interest to have a mistress, but any man who marries my daughter will not. Do you understand? She deserves happiness. If you wish to have an amicable relationship with me and anyone of my acquaintance, you will see that she is happy." Lord Pepperwirth waited for a reply, his arms folded across his chest.

Owen chose his words carefully. "She may not be who I would have chosen, but I will honor our vows and do everything in my power to make her happy." He had no plans of straying from his marriage bed and he wanted to make damned sure she didn't either by convincing her that being his wife and his lover would be intensely enjoyable. He valued the sanctity of marriage, even if he was a scoundrel in the eyes of polite society.

He meant it. If a marriage was to work, they both needed to be happy. And the challenge of seducing a fiery, temperamental woman who had a secret sensual side was fascinating.

"Good. Now"—Lord Pepperwirth stood and Owen rose as well—"Milly will have access to her dowry, as will you. I suggest you let her have charge of her finances as she needs them. My daughter spends wisely, and I desire her to have her freedom monetarily speaking, if she needs it."

Owen nodded. "That is fine, so long as she is amenable to helping me use a portion of it to help my estate."

Lord Pepperwirth walked halfway around his desk and then paused. "That's why you needed to marry, eh? My wife suspected money was a motive, but she guessed you had some vices to contend with. I don't approve if that's the course, but a man's land...that's another matter entirely."

There was no reason he had to tell Milly's father anything, but the man was owed a little bit of an explanation.

"Wesden Heath has been in my family for two hundred years. After my father passed while I was in South Africa for the war, it fell to my mother, and she couldn't keep up with it, not with her weak heart. She died a month before I came home. I want it to be a livable place again, a home for both Milly and me." Owen tugged at his jacket's sleeves, trying to look preoccupied should Pepperwirth have a negative response, but he didn't.

"Sounds like an honorable purpose, Mr. Hadley. Milly might be more useful to you than you know."

Such a vague promise from the older man! Owen raised his brows, hoping Pepperwirth would expand on his comment, but he was disappointed.

"Well, it's time we join the others. I'm famished after that ceremony."

Owen followed Milly's father out of the study and back into the dining room, where the ladies and a few close friends and family had gathered. Ivy and Leo separated themselves from the other guests and came over.

"Congratulations, Hadley." Leo's twinkling eyes held far too much delight at his expense for Owen to be happy.

"Yes, yes, have a good laugh," he muttered.

When Ivy shot a confused look between the two of them, Leo chuckled.

"Owen has never liked Mildred, and the same goes for her with him. Like a pair of tomcats in a sackcloth, hissing and biting." Leo's open mirth soured Owen's mood.

"You know full well I had other intentions."

At this Ivy scowled. "Yes, Leo mentioned that to me. Mr. Hadley, take my advice. Your taste for scandal has forced you to pay a high price. I suggest you take that lesson to heart." Her slightly almond-shaped eyes, so warm and dark with their Gypsy look, had once enchanted him. But they didn't any longer. Now when he pictured eyes, all he saw was blue flashing with fire and rebelliousness.

"Milly is sweeter than you realize, Mr. Hadley," Ivy continued, leaning into him as though not wishing to be overheard.

"Oh? That would surprise me." His reply was a little too sardonic because Leo harrumphed in disapproval. "What?" he challenged. "You aren't married to the woman. We're likely to kill each other before we even get to our honeymoon." While he was curious about Milly's behavior as a seductive challenge, he was not entirely ready to deal with the woman as a wife.

"She's very independent, Mr. Hadley. Don't cage her or she'll snap at you."

Cage her? That sounded like an impossible task. He shoved his hands into his trouser pockets and frowned.

"I have no intention of doing such a thing. She'll be perfectly free to do as she likes so long as it does not interfere with my affairs."

Leo rolled his eyes. "How romantic of you, Hadley. Come, Ivy dear, let's eat some cake." Leo steered her away as her face flushed and her lips parted as though she had something more to say. She'd likely have lectured him further if not for Leo's timely intervention.

Owen attempted to make small talk with the guests, but the niggling sense that he was somehow an outsider made him feel on edge. He wanted to fit into this world, the close community of the Hamptons and the Pepperwirths. Yet not a single person at the wedding aside from Leo had been here as his guest. Since his parents had died, he'd felt more alone than ever. Sure, he had a few distant cousins on the Hadley side, but none so close he could have invited to the wedding. It did not help matters that Milly seemed to be purposely avoiding him.

She'd come down after she'd changed, wearing a white blouse tucked into a sensible tweed skirt. The back and front panels of her skirt had buttons and trimmed braid along the hem. It displayed her small waist and the flare of her womanly hips in an elegant and all too pleasing style. Milly hadn't dressed to look risqué, yet he couldn't help but entertain delightfully wicked thoughts about getting his hands under her skirt. Even if she was flashing those blue eyes at him in anger, he'd do his best to tempt her to passion.

With a silent curse, Owen had to admit the woman was twisting him in confusing knots. He thought he didn't like her, but she kept making him change his mind —even when she seemed determined to frustrate him. One moment he wanted to drag her to bed. The next he wanted to go straight back to Brooks in London and avoid her until they learned to live together amicably. Was that even possible with Milly? He chuckled softly, drawing several confused looks from guests nearby. He cleared his throat and focused on the breakfast. All he wanted to do was get this over with and leave so he could sort out how he felt about his wife in private.

He'd secured a room at the White Rose Inn for a night's stay and it was going to be difficult enough getting Milly not to throw a fuss. But he was going to insist they share a room and a bed as man and wife, even if they did not consummate their marriage. At this rate that would likely take years. Not that he wouldn't do everything in his power to convince her that sharing a bed with him would be pleasurable. But no doubt in his first attempt to woo her, she'd want to strangle him. He knew she didn't want this marriage and she had quite a temper when she was riled.

He groaned. It would be sheer luck if his new wife didn't smother him with a pillow tonight while he slept.

Chapter Five

Milly hugged her parents goodbye and gave Rowena a kiss on the cheek. Rowena wiped tears from her eyes.

"Oh, Milly, you'll let me come visit you? Mama says once she's hired a lady's maid for me, she'll let me come and see you." Rowena hugged her again, her little nose turning red as she sniffled.

Milly glanced at Owen, who stood by the hired cab. "I'm sure that will be fine. I'll write to you and let you know once I'm settled."

"Good." Rowena stepped back, clutching her hands together, trying to smile, but it wobbled. Milly wanted to stay here, with her family, in a place she was familiar with and comfortable. She was heading off to the unknown tonight and not having any control was terrifying. She was married to a stranger, going to a town she'd never been to before, and she was so alone. Her stomach clenched in tight knots and her heart ached as she realized her life would never been the same.

"Ready?" Owen called out a little loudly from behind her. She flinched and gave her parents one last smile.

"You'll be fine, Milly. Write to us as soon as you can," her mother said, blinking away a suspicious sheen of tears in her eyes.

Milly pulled her coat tighter about her as she turned and walked over to the cab. She paused before she climbed inside, her heart clinging to one last moment of the life she'd known, and then with a sigh she entered the vehicle. The driver in the front seat had already loaded their travel cases and they were ready to leave. Milly scooted over to allow Owen inside. He sat down and told the driver to leave.

As the cab pulled away from Pepperwirth Vale, she turned in the seat to peer through the small window. The shrinking view of her former home shattered her heart. She was leaving everything and everyone she loved behind for a forced marriage. If she had been marrying a man she loved, and one who loved her, she still would have felt sad at leaving her home. But leaving it while being tied to a fortune hunter who would never see her value, never care about her heart or her mind or love her? It was too much to bear. Her bottom lip trembled and she bit it to keep it from showing. As she turned back round, she noticed Owen watching her, a solemn expression on his face.

"Are you all right?" he asked.

She blinked rapidly as her eyes burned. "Yes, quite fine," she replied crisply.

"Very well," he responded gruffly, and focused on something outside the cab window.

She regretted her tone, but it was too late to do anything about it. They had a long ride ahead of them. She fluffed the fur of her coat collar up higher on her neck and settled in to watch the passing scenery. She closed her eyes, only for a moment...

The cab rolled to a stop and the motion shook her awake. Milly was leaning not against the side of the vehicle but against the warm body of the man beside her. Owen. He had one arm around her shoulders and her head was tucked beneath his chin. He was resting his cheek against the crown of her hair, apparently having drifted off to sleep as well. Milly held still, her breath shallow as she took stock of the situation logically. Not an easy thing to do when her body was more than happy to remind her it was cozy and warm, and a little tingly too. Why did he, of all men, have to affect her like this? A devious little voice in her head laughed.

He is my husband...would it be so bad to enjoy this?

Yes. The man is a cad. A womanizer who ruined you and trapped you into marriage.

"Sir?" the cab driver prompted.

"What?" Owen jolted woke, then glanced down at her, her face reflecting her own sense of shock.

"My apologies," Owen muttered. He removed his arm from her shoulders and leaned forward to speak to the driver about where to leave the car until they needed him tomorrow. Then Owen helped her out of the cab.

Milly realized it was evening. The light of the sun was barely a razor-thin shred of pink dawning on the horizon. She'd dozed off for a length of time, then. In front of her was a quaint little two-story building. An inn, with a wooden painted sign of a white rosebush.

"This way," Owen said, taking her arm and tucking it into his as he led her to the door. They entered the cheery interior of the inn. Several tables were full of local folk who were dining and drinking. A man in the corner by the fire was entertaining the crowd with a lively fiddle. Owen approached the bar, where an older man was filling pints of ale.

"Good evening, Mr. Hunter. My wife and I have a room reservation under Hadley."

The man smiled. "Ahh, Mr. Hadley, me and the missus was just wondering when you'd turn up. Long journey eh?" Mr. Hunter turned his warm smile at Milly and she found herself returning a sheepish smile.

"Yes, very long," she agreed.

"Well"—Mr. Hunter slapped his bar towel on the

counter—"no worries about that. I'll take you straight up to your room and send a lad to fetch your luggage from the cab once it's parked out back. The missus will see some hot food and drink sent up to you as well." He walked over to a wooden plaque behind the bar that contained keys hanging from nails. The innkeeper plucked one brass key with a number on a silver tag attached to it.

"Follow me." Hunter led them to a set of stairs with worn carpets. They tramped up behind him and down a narrow hall, where he stopped at the middle room and unlocked the door.

"This here is your room. I'll see to the food and luggage. If you have need of anything, just come on down and find me." As he left them, he set the keys in Owen's hand.

"Thank you, Mr. Hunter." Owen spread an arm wide to indicate for Milly to enter the room ahead of him.

She entered but froze at the sight of the single bed.

"Owen—" She spun but ran into his chest and had to stumble back.

"What's the matter?" He caught her by the shoulders to steady her.

"There's only one bed," she pointed out with a panicked jerk of her head.

He nodded, not looking at all disturbed. "We're

married, Milly. If I had requested two rooms or even a pair of beds, it would have raised questions about us."

"But we are married. Why would questions worry you?" she asked.

"I didn't—" He rubbed a hand over his jaw and scowled. "I don't have to explain my decisions to you. Now, get out of your coat and I'll start a fire so you can warm up. You're freezing." He turned away to shut the door.

Milly would have bristled and said something waspish about him not having to explain his decisions, but she was cold and tired. Sliding her coat off her shoulders, she came over to the pair of chairs facing the fire and eased down onto the edge of the seat, leaning toward the cold, dark hearth. Owen swept his cap off his head and raked a hand through his dark hair as he knelt by the fireplace. She couldn't help but study his fine form as he located a box of matches and a set of kindling before he began to prepare the fire. Milly watched him, fascinated. Once little flames sparked and glowed over the soft kindling, Owen added several legs, hoping to spread the fire until it warmed the room with a healthy heat.

"How did you know how to do that?" she asked as he stood and gazed at the little clock on the mantel. Without looking at her, he retrieved his silver pocket watch from his waistcoat and checked the time against the watch. He opened the glass case and tweaked the minute hand before closing the glass and turning back to her.

"Know to do what?"

Milly gestured to the fire. "Make a fire. I don't know how to do that; my servants take care of lighting fires."

Owen walked over to the bed and retrieved a thick woolen blanket from the end of it. He then held the wool out in front of the fire for a few minutes before he approached her and settled the blanket around her body.

"What are you doing?"

He tucked the blanket firmly around her, then pressed her back into the chair so the hot blanket warmed her from neck to bottom. The singeing sensation against her skin burned her deliciously. When he didn't immediately reply, she decided to nudge him a little.

"Owen," she murmured, wishing he'd speak to her. The silence between them was unsettling.

He seated himself by the fire, arms resting on the chair arms as he gazed at the flames.

"I learned to make fires during the war."

His words pulled her out of her cozy contentment.

"The war?"

He nodded, finally glancing her way. There was pain in his eyes, and something about it sliced her heart to ribbons.

"I had two friends growing up—Leo, whom you've met, and Jack Watson."

"Jack?" In their dozens of conversations leading up the wedding, they had spoken lightly of their pasts and she hadn't heard Jack mentioned until now.

"Yes. Leo stayed home under orders from his parents, but Jack and I...we rushed off to be soldiers. What fools we were." He closed his eyes, rubbing the bridge of his nose. "We fought against the Boers. We were always on the move, columns of troops constantly deployed to South Africa, but whenever we left an area, the enemy troops came back. Out on the African plains, you learn to keep warm at night when the air turns colder than ice. Jack was our regiment's doctor, but I was more of a solider than Jack. I learned how to survive out there and made it my mission to take care of everyone, especially those closest to me. I didn't always succeed."

Something about his hollow tone made her chest ache.

Milly's lungs burned and when she inhaled, she realized she'd been holding her breath. Owen had been a soldier? She studied history, knew how hard the war had been, the guerrilla fighting, the destruction of innocent towns, the concentration camps. What could she say to a man who'd seen so much death and destruction?

"I'm sorry. I didn't know you'd fought in the war. It must have been very terrible. My father had friends who perished on the battlefield as well." It was a feeble attempt to soothe him, but what else could she have said?

Owen shrugged. "It was years ago." Yet the dark shadows behind his eyes said so much. "Jack suffers more from the memories than I do; he always had a bigger heart than me."

Milly studied her husband closely, wondering if that were true. There was something about the way he spoke of Jack that showed he cared about this other man, that friendships with Owen ran deep. It surprised her. She expected a man driven by money to not have strong loyalties or ties to anyone but himself.

There was a knock at the door. Owen stood and opened it, allowing a young man to enter. He carried two travel cases, one under each arm. Owen relieved him of one and helped the man set it on the bed. Behind him, a plump, sweet-faced lady bore a tray with a pair of covered plates, a pair of bowls, also covered, and a basket of fresh bread.

"Here you are, dears. Thought you might be a bit peckish after your journey." The woman, Mrs. Hunter, carried the tray over and set it down on the little table between the two chairs by the fire.

"If you need anything, you just come downstairs and I'll see to it." Mrs. Hunter winked at Milly, her bright smile a comfort in this strange place.

"Thank you, Mrs. Hunter," she said just before the woman and the young lad exited the room. Owen closed the door behind them and slid the latch into place, securing them in the room alone.

"Why did you lock us in?" she demanded, a little breathless with worry.

He grinned knowingly. "Sometimes men in their cups get a little adventurous. I don't want any drunken sods stumbling into our room while we sleep."

"Oh." She exhaled in relief. That made sense. She hadn't considered that.

He took his chair again and lifted the covers off the food. There was soup and shepherd's pie and warm bread, simple but enticing. Although she was used to elegant and extravagant meals, this hearty and simplistic fare didn't bother her at all. It smelled wonderful. Her stomach growled as she leaned close to the trays and inhaled the delicious aromas.

Owen divided the meal between the two of them and she settled the warm soup bowl in her lap, relishing the heat of the china against her cold hands.

"Milly." Owen said her name softly and she looked up at him. He was watching her with an insatiable gaze while one of his hands toyed with a spoon. His fingers were elegant, long, but beautiful in a masculine way. She'd never been alone with a man, and here she was, lost in fascination by his hands. A blush flared in her cheeks.

"Yes," she replied, then sipped her soup and tried to remain calm.

"We don't really know each other..." He cleared his throat. "At all."

She nodded. Their conversations prior to the wedding had always been chaperoned and light in topic. It was hard to learn about him that way and if they were to make this marriage work, which she hoped he wanted to as much as she did, getting to know him would help.

"I would like"—he paused, lingering on the word—"to know you more. I believe we should try to get a little acquainted. What do you think? We could make a game of it. You ask me anything you want, I'll give you a truthful answer, and then it's my turn. We can try it while we eat." He waited for her to answer and took two spoonfuls of soup.

A game? Getting to know him? They were trapped in this marriage, and she didn't like the idea of being lonely. Perhaps he could make this amusing.

"I think I can play the game." She gave him a small smile. Why did that make her feel so vulnerable? Offering this man, her husband, a smile...

"Excellent." He grinned again and something in her lower belly quivered.

I shouldn't like his smile. But I do. Lord help me, I do.

"Shall I ask the first question?" she volunteered, and dipped some of her bread into the thick soup, soaking it up before she nibbled on the slice.

Owen chuckled. "You may."

She studied him for a long while, then asked her question. "What do you love about Wesden Heath?" She'd heard it mentioned, had seen its listing as his major landholding, but hadn't been there or to the Cotswolds before, where she knew Wesden Heath was located.

Owen's eyes softened and his smile was so tender it surprised her.

"Wesden Heath is full of color. That's what I love most about it. It is full of wildflowers, and everything is green most of the year, save deep winter. When I came back from fighting, it was the only place that left me feeling safe." He chuckled softly. "I suppose that makes me sound foolish, but it's true. It's why I love my home."

Milly held her breath, stunned to see clear on his face and hear in his voice the truth of that. If he was after money to save a home that had saved him...She tried to bury the rush of sympathy for him that arose inside her in that moment. Thankfully, he laughed and spoke again.

"Oh, and there are the Cotswold lion sheep. I loved our herds, when we raised them."

"Lion sheep?" she asked, leaning toward him curiously.

"That's a new question. It's my turn." He waggled a finger at her, then reached for his glass of wine and sipped.

Milly had never heard of lion sheep and she was delighted at the way the game was playing so far; there was a strange anticipation to waiting to learn more about him.

"What is your favorite novel?" he asked.

The question surprised her. "Novel? Well, I recently finished J. M. Barrie's *Peter and Wendy*. It's fairly new, only published last week. Have you heard of it?"

Owen set aside his soup bowl and tucked into his shepherd's pie. "Barrie. He's a playwright, isn't he? I believe I remember the play but didn't know he'd written a novel. What do you like about Barrie's book?"

This time it was Milly's turn to waggle a finger at him. "Oh no, it's my turn now. What are lion sheep?" She forgot her sense of decorum as they talked and she lifted her skirts to tuck her legs up underneath her in a curled position on the chair.

"Oh, you little clever creature," he teased with a merry twinkle. "Very well, the lion sheep." He went on to describe them, and she realized how crucial they were. A staple of the Cotswolds area for wool and food.

"They're tall beasts, and extremely intimidating," Owen finished, but Milly burst out laughing in delight.

"Sheep intimidating? How so?"

Owen handed her a glass of wine. "Trust me, when you see one, you'll understand exactly what I mean. Now, why do you like *Peter and Wendy*?"

She sipped her wine, relishing the way it spread warmth all the way through her.

"It's a tragic story really, about a little girl who falls in love with a boy who will never grow up."

Owen propped one arm on his chair. "I thought the book was about the boy?"

Milly shook her head. "You might think so, but it is really about the girl, Wendy Darling. How she finds love, then must abandon her childhood and her dreams, which are represented by Peter. She has to grow up. The plight of all women." She glanced away, feeling suddenly foolish for trying to explain something that she had understood on a deeply personal level. She'd had to abandon her own dreams of love and freedom when she'd returned home from school in France and realized that living with a husband as an equal would likely never be possible. The husbands of England weren't accepting and respectful of women as equals, not to the extent that she'd seen in France. Having to face that any man she married would see her as "less" even if he claimed to love her had broken her heart. It didn't stop her from secretly hoping she'd find a man someday who would prove her wrong, but now it was too late.

"I suppose we men make it seem like we never grow up," Owen said, his voice a little gruff as he once again stared at the fire. "But some of us do, at great cost."

"You mean the war, don't you?" she asked.

He nodded, his gaze meeting hers. "When you've tasted blood and taken lives, it leaves scars that never heal. I haven't gone a single night without nightmares since I came home and it's been years."

There was such hurt in his eyes that Milly reached across the small table to rest her hand on his before she even realized what she was doing. He stared at their connection for a long moment and before she could pull away, he turned his hand over, so his palm touched hers and curled his fingers around hers, squeezing gently. The touch, so affectionate, tender, and genuinely unexpected from a man like him sent ripples of shock through her.

"Have you had enough to eat?" He nodded at her mostly empty plate.

"Yes," she said. At this, she withdrew her hand from his and set her dishes back on the tray.

"Let me prepare a few foot warmers while you change."

"Change?" For a second she didn't comprehend his words. "Oh, you mean..." She flushed when he smiled that dazzling smile at her, the one that cost too many ladies their reputations.

"I wouldn't want you to be uncomfortable tonight."

Milly sucked in a breath. "Are you going to...Are we..." How was she supposed to ask him if he would make love to her?

Owen stood and walked over to her, placing one palm on the back of the chair beside her head and he leaned over to cup her chin with his free hand. The pad of his thumb brushed over her lips, caressing them, his hypnotic gaze focused on her mouth.

"Whatever you think of me, Milly, know this: I am not a villain. I would never force you. One day, I hope we'll like each other enough to try, but I know you still have reservations."

Reservations? She didn't think that was the right word at all. She was terrified of the idea of him pinning her down on the bed so he could take his pleasure. Her mother had whispered a little conspiratorially that sometimes if a man was skilled, he could give a woman pleasure, but most men did not. It was often uncomfortable and occasionally painful. It didn't sound at all like something she'd like to do, even if Owen's mere touch and sinful gaze did strange things to her heart and her body.

"I...am not ready." She hated her own cowardice, but the idea of that intimacy frightened her. It was impossible to miss the disappointment shadowing his eyes as he swallowed hard and then nodded.

"Then you are safe tonight. We must share the bed, but I will not touch you." He turned away and something inside her felt as though it had shriveled and died.

Why can't I be brave? She was so strong in everything else...but when it came to a man, a man she hated to admit she desired, she was lost, insecure.

"Why don't you change?" He resting one hand on the mantel of the fireplace as he stoked the logs with a black poker. He cut such a fine figure, with tall straight legs and narrow hips, a contrast to his broad shoulders. He was like a powerful ancient god trapped in mortal flesh. Beautiful in the way some men could be.

Milly forced herself to get up from the chair and go to her travel valise. She unlocked the clasps and dug through the contents until she found her nightdress. It was a beautiful lace creation with ribbon insertions, but was thick enough to keep her warm. She looked over her shoulder at Owen. He was still focused on the fire. There was nowhere to hide, no changing room or dressing gown. Milly stared down at her clothes and then with a silent curse, she pulled her blouse out from her skirt and lifted it over her head. Then she unbuttoned the tweed skirt and let it drop. She still wore a corset and her chemise, but she needed help getting out of them.

"Owen, could you...help me?" She clutched the thick nightgown to her breasts, concealing them as much as she could while she waited. When he turned around, his gaze darkened as he took in her appearance.

"My corset..." Offering her back to him, she held her breath, listening to the sound of his booted steps on the floor behind her.

His fingers touched the laces, tugging, then sliding as he loosened and pulled them. The rasping of the laces against his skin and the crackle of the fire were the only sounds in the room, save for the faint panting breaths that escaped her lips.

"There, all done," he whispered, but didn't move

away. One hand settled on her bare shoulder and toyed with the strap of her chemise in gentle, little strokes. That single point of contact sent ripples of fire across her skin down to her toes, and the secret spot between her legs zinged with a sharp, strange pang.

"Would you let me have one good night kiss?" His voice was rough and low. The sound of it scraped deliciously against her skin.

A kiss? One kiss wouldn't hurt.

Before she could second-guess her judgment, she turned to face him, her nightdress still clutched to her breasts like a shield. The angular line of his strong jaw was outlined by shadows from the firelight. His lips were slightly parted and his dark lashes fanned down to half-mast. She licked her lips, recalling the way he'd tasted the last time they'd kissed. How exquisite it felt to be in his arms, surrendering to waves of passion. Would it feel that way again?

"God how you tempt me," he growled. It was her only warning before he dragged her into his embrace and slanted his mouth over hers.

Milly dropped the nightgown in shock and then clasped her hands on Owen's shoulders as he coaxed her lips apart. His tongue thrust boldly between her lips and she moaned when it playfully danced against her own. The way he moved his lips, the way their breaths were shared in that small space between them seemed to bind them together in a dream. It was a hazy, warm dream that made desire and hunger for dark wicked things coil heatedly in her belly. She stood up on tiptoe, trying to get closer to him, to taste more of him, devour him in any way she could.

His large, strong hands explored her shoulders, traced her shoulder blades, and then tangled in the loosened laces of her corset. He was nearly ready to rip it off her, but he suddenly halted, his mouth leaving hers as he forced himself back a step. The action felt like a slap. Milly bit her kiss-swollen lips, hating that she wanted him to keep kissing her and despising that she missed his touch after only seconds. It wasn't right to want him like this, to want the things her body seemed to crave after only a few kisses. She now understood why men like Owen were fatal to a woman's reputation. She would do just about anything to stay in his arms.

"You should finish undressing." He cleared his throat again and then without looking her way he went over to his own suitcase and stared digging around in its contents.

Milly watched for a few moments as he stripped out of his coat and started to unbutton his shirt. The sight of his bare chest through the partially open shirt was so distracting that she continued to stare until Owen chuckled.

"If you want to see me undress, you need only ask." He grinned wickedly. "It is your right as my wife."

Milly blinked and came back to herself. His ability to burn hot and then cold was so confusing. One minute he was asking to kiss her and the next he was pulling away.

She hastily turned her back on him and finished removing her corset. The filmy chemise was next. She tried not to think about the fact that Owen could see her entirely nude backside as she lifted the chemise up and off her body.

"Ready for bed, wife?" Owen's voice was rich, seductive, and pure temptation.

Lord help me, how will I survive this night?

Chapter Six

Owen couldn't get the sight of Milly's bare backside out of his mind. She was, in a word, stunning. The flare of her hips, the hourglass figure, the curve of her buttocks. He was hard from the single glimpse of her before the nightdress dropped down, covering her. The edge of his control was fraying at the ends. That kiss had been explosive, and his hands still trembled with the need to touch her, to explore every inch of her. It was going to be a miracle if he survived sleeping in bed beside her. The idea that Milly, of all the ladies in England, would tempt him should have been laughable and yet he couldn't deny that he was fascinated by her.

Since the moment he'd taken her away from her home, she'd seemed a different woman, one so alone, scared, yet she was holding her chin up bravely. He'd seen the glimmer of tears in her eyes when they'd driven away from Pepperwirth Vale and his heart had gone out to her. It brought back too many memories of how he'd felt when he and Jack had departed England. When he'd left Wesden Heath and sat beneath an African sun fighting a war that blackened his heart, it had nearly destroyed him. After he'd returned home to find both his parents dead and his home in shambles, he'd been unable to recover a part of himself that seemed to have died too. His father's debts had crippled the estate and he'd barely been able to keep it afloat these last few years. He'd heard it once said that when a woman married, it was like she was going off to war. With him, it was certainly war, since she didn't like him at all...except when they were kissing, that is. When they kissed, she seemed to like him quite well. He bit his lip to hide a grin.

"Owen." Milly's soft, husky voice pulled him from his thoughts.

She was standing by the fire now, lifting the hot foot warmers and carrying them carefully to the bed. She nodded at him to draw the blankets back and he hastily did so. She tucked the warmers into the foot of the bed and then crawled in under the covers. Her eyes, so rich in color and so wide with appreciation, tore at his heart. She was brave to be here with him, to agree to go with him by herself. Marriage did not equal trust or intimacy. No, those things had to come more slowly, more gently with time spent together. The shrewish nature she'd displayed was not who she truly was. He was figuring her out now, bit by bit, and he was seeing the real Milly underneath her bluster and standoffishness.

Her hair was still bound up in a pile on her head and he knew she'd forgotten it. He couldn't help but admire the way it showed the graceful slope of her neck and how a few stray curls fell down to touch her throat. As beautiful as the hairstyle was, though, he knew the pins would be uncomfortable to sleep in.

He finished stripping out of his shirt and trousers while she turned her head away discreetly. After he'd donned his sleeping pants, he approached the bed.

"Milly, your hair is still—"

She reached up to touch it, instantly wincing. "Oh yes, I forgot." She began to feel about blindly for the pins.

"Allow me." He climbed onto the bed and reached for her hair. She stared at him; then after a long moment, she scooted forward in the bed and gave him her back. He knelt behind her, his knees sliding around her hips as he got close enough to see her hair. The rich chestnut locks were coiled on her head and he started pulling pins out. With each pin removed, a lock of hair tumbled down her back. The silken tresses tickled her skin as he threaded his fingers through them, searching for more pins.

A sigh escaped Milly's lips as he massaged her scalp with little strokes.

"That feels nice," she admitted in a whisper.

"Do you want me to stop?" he asked.

A pause, then, "No, at least not yet." She shifted, sitting in a more comfortable position, and one of her hands brushed over his thigh. He tensed as his body responded, hunger for her coiling inside him. Lord, he wanted Milly on her back beneath him so he could—

Owen gave a little shake and forced all the wicked thoughts of bedding his wife out of his head. It wasn't easy. Not when her hand still touched him, so close to where he wanted her to really touch him, with her hands, her mouth...With a silent growl at himself, he resumed the light massage of her head, rubbing her temples, then her neck and shoulders before he finally let his hands drop.

"Feel better?"

"Much." She looked over her shoulder at him, the movement sending her hair in a ripple down her back.

"Good. I'll turn out the lamps and check the fire once more before I turn in."

She cuddled down beneath the blankets, her eyes hunting him as he moved about the room. He turned the little knobs on the lamps, dousing them, then added a few more logs to the fire before climbing into bed. The space between him and Milly wasn't much, but he liked being close to her when she wasn't acting as prickly as a hedgehog. Owen pulled the blankets up around them and settled in on his pillow. She turned her head enough that the moonlight illuminated the curve of her cheek and the shape of her lips. He'd thought Rowena would have suited him as a wife. But after being around Milly, kissing her, listening to her talk about literature, he'd realized that a woman who was closer to him in age, and not just coming out in society, was a better match. She had lived more, understood more than a young lady like Milly's little sister would. In a way, she was more suited to him than he ever could have imagined.

There was so much he wanted to say, to tell her, but fear kept him silent. Would she despise him for admitting that he was glad he'd compromised her and not Rowena? She would likely hate him for it. He couldn't let her know how much she affected him. Unable to resist one little touch, he stroked her arm with his fingertips. She was tense, almost rigid, and he didn't want her to be. He wanted her to feel at ease.

"Get some rest. We will have to rise early tomorrow to reach Wesden Heath."

She exhaled softly and turned her head deeper into the pillow, depriving him of the tempting sight of her cheek, the flutter of her long lashes.

"Good night...husband," she said. He continued to stroke her and she didn't pull away.

"Good night, wife." He was still smiling in the dark as he closed his eyes.

I SLEPT WITH MY HUSBAND.

It was the first thought Milly had upon waking to find herself locked in the warm embrace of Owen's arms. Sometime in the night she had rolled over to face him and he'd wrapped his arms around her. His chest was bare and her cheek was pressed to his hot skin. Her hands were tucked up between her body and his and she was able to lightly touch his chest. Giving it a featherlight stroke, she glanced up, hoping he wouldn't wake.

In that moment, his large body enveloped hers in a warm bed surrounded by faint morning sunlight. She was safe and content. The dream she'd been afraid to hope for seemed to be within reach. She knew logically that this man was not someone who would treat her equally or love her, not in the way she'd secretly hoped her future husband would. Fortune hunters saw women only for the value of money they brought to a man. She knew enough of those sort of men from her past seasons in London, including the rumors she'd heard about Owen, to be sure that they cared little for the rights of women and certainly never fell in love with them. But for just a short while, she was going to pretend it was possible that Owen might care about her, that he might love her and value her as a person.

"Did you sleep well?" His question startled her out of

her thoughts and she jolted away from him. He was awake, had been awake for who knew how long. Shame at being caught stroking his chest, cuddling with him, filled her like a handful of heavy stones.

"Milly, don't do that." His little sigh of exasperation made her bristle with frustration.

"Do what? I'm not doing anything." She scooted back a foot, but the blankets tangled around her legs and his. They were trapped in together, which moments ago had been delightful, but now she saw the potential problem. She couldn't get free if he didn't help her.

Owen propped his head in his hand against the pillow and stared down at her, his lips twitching as though he was fighting the urge not to laugh.

"You act as though touching me is something to be ashamed of." He sobered and toyed with a lock of her hair by her cheek. As he did so, he moved his leg, just enough that it shifted between her own. His knee bumped hers, nudging her legs farther apart. Her nightdress was bunched up around her thighs. She'd always kicked up the dress in her sleep and last night was no different, except a man was sharing her bed, had easier access to her...

"It isn't, you know," he continued, "bad for you to touch me." He released the curl of her hair and covered one of her hands with his. He stroked a fingertip over the back of her hand, tracing the fine veins there before he raised his gaze to hers. When he did, she forgot to breathe.

There was so much in his eyes that she was afraid of. If she fell for this darkly handsome man with laughing eyes, it would destroy her. He didn't love her, nor would he likely ever love her in the way she'd secretly dreamed of. She didn't want to play a servant to a man's whims and be his property; she wanted a man to love her for her mind and heart and see her as something *more*...She was terrified Owen would never be that man for her.

Heat, passion, lust, a hint of something hot, and a flicker of darkness, too, left her heart beating wildly and her body shaking. He made her feel so much of that fire with only a gaze. She wasn't ready to experience what he was offering, because if she gave in to temptation and let herself go with him, she would be that much closer to falling in love.

He turned her hand over, baring her palm; then he continued to touch her, creating little swirl lines on her skin. A moment later, he lifted her hand to his lips and kissed it. It singed her skin and a trembling of longing rolled through her, shortly followed by a sharp stab of arousal between her thighs. She clenched her knees together instinctively, which only clamped his leg between hers, keeping them locked together.

"You may touch me anytime you wish," Owen said. "Anywhere, anytime. I'm your husband. It's not something you need ever be afraid or ashamed of." There was such an earnest feeling to his words that her resolve to avoid him began to quake and crumble. With a delicate slowness, she curled her hand up so her fingers clasped his.

Her lips parted and the words were there, on the tip of her tongue, but she couldn't get them out.

Please don't hurt me. Don't make me regret trusting you. She silently begged him not to crush her spirit; it would be so easy to fall for him. And it wasn't just because he made her feel good physically. It was the small things, like warming a blanket for her by the fire and asking her questions about books over dinner. As much as she wanted to paint him a blackguard and a fortune hunter, she couldn't deny that his actions spoke against her poor opinion of him.

This was why she feared falling for a man who wouldn't treat her as an equal. Owen had tried to seduce other women with the intent to marry for money, but with her he'd actually succeeded. He was the exact opposite of a man who would see her value and her partnership in a marriage. Yet Owen was just the sort of man to entrap her heart. Beneath those wicked smiles and playful kisses was a tortured, lonely soul, damaged by war and loss. She wasn't a fool. She could see the pieces of himself he'd struggled to put back together. He had almost convinced her he was a heartless man who went from conquest to conquest with no thought to the woman he'd bedded. But that was an act. Owen Hadley, at least the man she'd first met, was an imposter. The real Owen lay beside her in bed, and she was still puzzling him out. Who was the real Owen? What demons haunted him in the dead of night? What secrets did he try to bury?

There was something more to him and his motivations but she couldn't figure it out. What advantage did he gain in seducing her? She and her fortune already belonged to him in every legal way that mattered. His every touch, every kiss and lingering gaze that heated her blood made little sense. Was he determined to steal her heart as well?

Milly lost count of the minutes as they lay in bed together, staring at each other, hands linked, legs locked. It was only after a long while that Owen spoke.

"We should get out of bed. I'll have breakfast brought up while you see to your needs." He was the first to break that slowly building connection and she regretted the loss of his touch. He removed himself from the bed and reached for his robe.

Milly waited until he was changed and out of the room before she slipped out from under the bedclothes and washed her face at the basin of cold water on the dresser. The icy splash on her heated skin felt good and jolted her into awareness. It erased the thick warmth she had inside at the thought of crawling back into bed and enticing Owen to join her. What a terrible idea! Milly gave herself a little reprimanding shake of the head.

She didn't bother with a bath; she could do that

when they reached Wesden Heath that evening. Running her brush through her hair, she combed out the tangles and fastened it into a loose knot at the base of her neck and secured it in with pins. A few stray wisps escaped in flyaways near her temples, but they couldn't be helped. After she searched her luggage, she found a new navy blue coat with braided black trim and a fresh blouse. She stripped out of her nightdress and pulled on fresh stockings and underclothes before she turned to stare at her corset, which lay across the rumpled bedsheets.

She never dreamed she'd dare go without it, but she didn't want to ask Owen to help her get into it. With a little growl of frustration, she stuffed it in her travel case and finished dressing. When she was done, she studied her appearance in the small mirror above the dresser. It didn't look too obvious that her breasts were unbound. The skirt was a little tight around her waist, but she could breathe much easier without the whalebone crushing her ribs.

"Well, it's not as if he'll notice," she muttered just as the door opened. Owen strolled inside, his gaze boldly raking over her.

"Won't notice what?" he asked.

Milly shook her head, swallowed, and glanced away, but she could feel the creeping heat in her cheeks.

"Nothing," she murmured, and hastily locked her travel case. Constance would blister her ears for such a mess of the clothes squashed inside but Milly would have to endure it.

"Ready? Breakfast is downstairs." Owen held out a hand and Milly accepted it, despite every instinct warning her to stay away from the man who could break her heart if given the chance.

As they came down the stairs into the common room, Mrs. Hunter waved them over to a table.

"Here, dears, have a seat." She gestured to a cozy little table just big enough for two. The common room was empty of the boisterous crows of the previous night and was filled instead with lodgers quietly enjoying their morning breakfast.

"Thank you, Mrs. Hunter," Milly said as Owen helped her to sit before he took his own chair across from her.

"We're so happy to have you here. Mr. Hunter says newlyweds are good luck." She winked at them and left them to eat.

"Make sure you get enough to eat. Cook won't have made much for dinner and I don't want you to go hungry tonight."

Owen's statement froze Milly in place, her hand hovering over a tray of johnnycake with potatoes. "You mean..." She paused, reached for the pot of coffee, and helped herself before continuing. "We need to fill the larder at the house?" What sort of self-respecting cook would let the stores get so low that they couldn't support even two people for dinner? Maybe Owen's debts on the estate were truly high enough that he couldn't keep the household running properly. Was the household that bad off that the larders were empty? The thought made her shiver.

Owen didn't meet her gaze as he filled a plate with eggs, bacon, and some steamed finnan haddie, a delicious fish that Milly had always enjoyed at home. The presence of the dish here at a small inn was a surprise.

"The haddie was made special for us. Want a bite?" Owen chuckled when he noticed her staring at the dish with longing.

"Yes, please." She offered her plate. "Now about the kitchen—"

"We'll see to that once you're settled into your rooms at Wesden Heath." Owen's tone wasn't sharp, but she had the distinct impression she'd somehow been reprimanded and knew by the cool look he gave her that he would not discuss the matter any further this morning.

She wanted to lay into him and tell him how wretched he was for refusing to answer her questions, but being churlish would achieve nothing. If he wanted to play that particular game, then she would, too...only, she would win.

After breakfast, the hired cab was pulled around, their luggage loaded, and she and Owen were back in the cab together, riding along toward his home in complete silence. To pass the time, she read a book and thankfully was lost in the story until something tapped the book's spine repeatedly. She lifted her head and saw Owen's hand was inches away, fingers rapping lightly on her book's cover. She shot him a mutinous glare.

"I like it when you wrinkle your nose. It's rather adorable, you know." He leaned back and crossed his arms over his chest.

"I do not wrinkle my nose. Good heavens, a lady would never—"

"Spare me whatever ladies would never do. I have no interest in dying of tedium. Now, what is that you're reading? You've been so engrossed in it we're nearly home. About eight miles is all."

Milly blinked and looked out at the late afternoon sun kissing the tops of the trees in the western sky.

"It's been that long?" She started to close the book but Owen deftly snapped it out of her hands, reading the title.

"*She* by H. Rider Haggard." He flipped through it, skimming a few pages. "What is it about?"

Milly would have ignored him, but she loved talking about literature. The few suitors in the past who had tried to talk to her had always discussed fashion and other nonsense, as though they didn't believe she could converse on anything else. Books were the way to her heart, not clothes.

"Two Englishmen venture into Africa and stumble upon a lost kingdom. The queen, Ayesha, or She Who Must be Obeyed, takes a fancy to the younger of the two gentlemen."

Owen chuckled. "She who must be obeyed? Now I understand your fascination. Women with the need to control and dominate men must stick together, eh?"

The comment was meant to be teasing she supposed, but it felt barbed, like the prickle of a cocklebur against her skin. He thought she wanted to control and dominate him? She didn't; she merely wanted to assert control over her own life and not be the puppet of a man. Tears of anger and something else she didn't want to admit to stung her eyes and she looked out the window away from him. She wanted to verbally lash out, but she didn't wish to do it in front of the driver.

"It is no concern of mine if you fail to see the broader aspects of literature," she replied icily. Then, mastering her face, she turned back to him and held out a gloved hand. "Please return my book to me."

He held it out, but the moment she reached for it, he moved fast. Wrapping an arm around her waist, he pinned her back against the seat.

"I didn't mean to hurt you, Milly. Never think that my teasing is to that end. I can be a bloody fool when I'm not thinking clearly." He was close enough that his warm breath fanned her cheeks and she had trouble focusing on anything but how soft his lips looked as he spoke. He was apologizing in his own way; she saw the regret in his eyes, only just tempering a heated passion she was beginning to recognize.

Her breath quickened as he reached up to brush the backs of his fingers against her cheek. The tenderness of it made her tremble in his arms. A cruel-hearted fortune hunter wouldn't touch her like this, would show such a soft side. Realizing this made her shake even harder as her heart clenched and her body heated. His eyes were warm as they gazed upon her, and desire was there mixed with something else she was afraid to hope for. She had to speak, had to break this slowly building enchantment he was casting over her.

"You are a fool quite often," she replied, but her tone was husky. When his gaze strayed to her lips, she knew he wanted to kiss her and she knew that she wanted that kiss, too.

"That I am." He gave her time to fight him, to resist the inevitable kiss, but she didn't.

Arching her back to get closer, she curled her fingers around the lapels of his coat, tugging him into her. The kiss this time felt different...She wanted it as much as he did, and she had been furious with him for being so thoughtless, for saying things without thinking. She nipped his lips and a throaty little growl escaped his mouth. The primal sound startled her, and she couldn't escape him, not even if she wanted to.

The way he kissed was sinful, scandalous, as though he was determined to explore every inch of her mouth, to learn the way she tasted. Milly wanted to know the same about him and loved it when he opened his mouth, letting his tongue and hers flick and stroke against each other, but then it changed...He thrust his tongue repeatedly into her mouth, in a way that liquefied her entire body. A wave of heat rolled through, filling her mind with a strange fog. Her breasts felt heavy, and aching. She needed...A large hand covered her left breast, squeezing it.

"Where's your corset?" His low chuckle teased her as he nibbled that special spot just below her ear.

"Couldn't put it on without help." How she was able to get those words out when he was caressing her erect nipple through the thin layers of her blouse and chemise, she would never know.

"Little minx, I like that about you." He was teasing, but this time Milly refused to let it upset her. Maybe to him being a minx was a good thing? It did feel wonderful to let go and embrace this wildness that seemed to run through her like quicksilver. It took everything in her not to crawl into his lap and press every inch of herself against him. She'd never known she could be like this; she'd longed and dreamed she would be, with the right man, but she'd lost hope of that after her first London Season. Owen made her forget how she'd closed herself up to the world; he made her feel like a flower tasting the kiss of the sun for first time in centuries.

"God, I love how you taste," he moaned against her lips.

She gripped his hair, loving that it was long enough to thread her fingers through and grasp.

"Do you always talk so much?" She nibbled his bottom lip, exploring its sensual shape with her tongue.

"Not if you want my mouth to do other things." The sensual purr and everything his words could mean made her shiver. He lifted her legs into his lap, his free hand sliding up underneath her skirts and pausing at her upper thighs to play with the silk ribbons of her stockings. The teasing touches tore a hungry moan from her and she kissed him. Hard. A wetness pooled between her thighs and she shifted restlessly, trying to encourage him to move his hand higher.

A loud pop and a sudden jerk sent Milly and Owen flying forward. Owen threw out a hand, smacking it hard against the back of the front seat, his other hooked around her waist, keeping them both from getting injured by colliding with the seat in front of them.

"What the devil?" he growled. "Driver, what's happened?"

Milly clung to Owen as she tried to clear the fog in her head and make sense of her position. On Owen's lap, her skirts rucked up to her knees, her hair a messy tangle.

Good heavens...

"Sorry, sir. It seems we ruptured a tire on the motorcar." The driver climbed out of the cab and tossed his hat on the seat, then walked around the vehicle to assess the damage.

"Well, hell." Owen laughed. "If not for the tire, we might have forgotten where we were." This comment was more of a musing to himself than to her.

Milly was suddenly self-conscious again, and she tried in vain to fix her hair and jerk her skirts down. Her cheeks flamed and she retrieved her book from the floor of the cab and clutched it like a shield to her chest. Her heart was racing, the frantic beat so hard she felt it clear to the tips of her toes. She had never let herself act so freely, and half of her was caught up in the sheer delight of it while the other half of her wanted to crawl into a cave and hide to protect herself from how exposed she felt kissing Owen.

Owen got out of the car and walked over to the driver, his hands tucked in his trouser pockets as he and the driver studied the front tire. Milly noticed his dark hair was mussed and a light breeze kept ruffling it. The strands had been soft and thick, and touching them had been...exciting. Seeing the way she'd left her mark on him, even in a small way, was oddly satisfying.

He is my husband. I can kiss him whenever I wish,

can't I?

Owen kicked the tire with his shoe tip and then after a few more words with the driver, he opened the door to the backseat. He braced one hand on the roof of the car as he leaned toward her.

"Milly, sweetheart, we have to walk the rest of the way. We don't have any means to get to Wesden Heath tonight except by foot. Can you make it? The driver says we're about seven miles from the estate."

"We have to walk the entire way?" She glanced around at the rolling hills of green landscapes. In the distance a few thatched roof cottages could be seen.

Owen frowned slightly. "We might have to. Unless we can find a local farmer who could take us the remainder of the journey." He offered her a hand and she took it, letting him assist her out of the cab. She clutched the book, not wanting to leave it behind.

"What about our luggage?" she asked.

Owen glanced over at the driver, then back at her. "He will bring it tomorrow, or we can try to carry it."

Milly weighed the options. Constance should be settled at Wesden Heath with most of her clothing.

"I think I can manage without it," she replied.

The gleam of approval in his eyes filled her with warmth.

"Very well, let's get started. We have a long walk ahead of us."

Chapter Seven

Seven miles was a long way for a well-bred lady to walk on a country road in dainty black boots, but Milly made not one peep of protest or uttered one complaint. Owen had to bite his lip to keep from grinning. She was so...different than he'd thought. The Milly he'd thought he'd known had been an arrogant, cold-hearted young woman. And it was all a mask.

The real Milly was passionate, intelligent, and determined. But she was frightened of him, not physically but emotionally. He couldn't forget the way she'd looked when he'd teased her about her book. She had dared to open up to him about how she liked reading about strong female characters, but he'd said something he shouldn't have and rather than lash out, she'd retreated. He recognized that type of behavior only too well. He'd done the same with his father when they'd quarreled. She was starting to care about his opinions, and thinking he didn't like something hurt her. Owen and his father had never seen eye to eye on anything, and every fight had cost him part of his heart.

I'm going to have to be careful with her. Prove to her that she can trust me, that I do value what she says.

The revelation surprised him. He'd never dared to let a woman influence him before.

"How are you holding up?" he asked as they reached a small stone bridge that crossed a narrow stream. White geese toddled ahead of them, honking and squawking.

He didn't miss the flash of pain on Milly's face as she walked, or the slight limp on her right foot, as though she'd gotten hurt. They couldn't be far now. This stream abutted his property.

"I'm fine." Her response came out through gritted teeth.

Owen didn't like knowing she was hurting. It was his job to protect her.

"We have half a mile..." He paused by the bridge and caught her by the arm.

"Why are we stopping?" She glanced down at his hand on her arm.

"Why don't you rest for a minute?" He patted the gray stone of the bridge.

She looked ready to protest, so he gripped her by the waist and hoisted her up to sit her on the bridge's edge.

"Oh!" She clutched at him, shooting a panicked glance over her shoulder at the little stream below.

"I've got you," he soothed gently.

She leaned into him, not letting go of his arms. Neither of them spoke for a minute. The babbling noise of the water traveling through the green rushes on the river's edge was calming. A familiar sound, one he'd grown up with all this life.

"It's so peaceful here," Milly admitted, her expression softening as she watched the setting sun.

"It is," he agreed. The Cotswolds had always been a place of magic, the way the hills seemed to cocoon the little houses and the gardens in a tiny, protected sphere. Time did not tick into the future here. Except for the seasons changing, Owen would have sworn that this part of England never aged.

"Do you spend much time at Wesden Heath now? Or do you prefer London?" Milly asked.

He forced his gaze away from a family of ducks parading down the chilly edge of the stream's bank. "The last few years it's been London, but"—he paused, meeting her gaze at last—"I would like to call Wesden Heath home again, now that I have the ability to properly run the estate."

"Because of my dowry," Milly surmised. She didn't

seem surprised, but he saw that flash of pain again and he cursed himself.

"I will not lie to you, Milly. It was my motivation for finding a wife." He cupped her cheek and traced her bottom lip with his thumb. She brushed his hand away and looked away. That hurt him. It shouldn't but it did.

"I suppose it could be worse. At least you don't seem prone to vices, besides women." The last part of this was added with a touch of bitterness. For some reason that angered him.

"I made a promise to your father that I would not take other women to my bed. Only you, Milly. Do not throw my past lovers in my face. They no longer concern what lies between us." She had to understand that he meant it. He was a man bound by his word.

Her head whipped back around to face him, fire sparking in her eyes.

"What lies between us?" She jabbed a gloved fingertip into his chest. "What exactly *lies* between us?" Her tone was civil but there was a bite to it he didn't miss.

Owen scowled down at his wife, torn between the desire to kiss her or turn her over his knee. The woman was exasperating. She drove him in two different directions when she verbally sparred with him, and he couldn't figure out how to engage her without quarreling or kissing her.

"I have no bloody idea what's happening between us,

but I thought things were improving." His tone was just as cool but he was barely controlling that desire to grab her and kiss her to remind her just what he felt and how she felt about him.

Her nose wrinkled and she kicked out, her dainty boot striking his knee. Then she hissed in pain and reached down to hold her right foot. The action caused her to wobble and almost fall off the little bridge. He reacted quickly, scooping her up into his arms, catching her behind the back and under her knees.

"What are you doing?" She wriggled in the cradle of his arms and he laughed.

"Stop squirming. I'm going to carry you the rest of the way."

Her lips parted in shock and she blinked several times. "Put me down. I don't need to be carried. What if someone sees us? It would be highly improper."

"I'm not concerned about propriety. I'm more concerned about you." Owen started walking, easily holding her in his arms. She was a solid weight, but not heavy. He gazed down at her. "Do your feet still hurt?"

Her hesitation told him everything he needed to know.

"I'm trying to help you, sweetheart. Don't be so bloody stubborn."

"Stubborn?" she almost shrieked. "Oh! Put me down, you cad!"

"You're hurt and I'm not letting my wife walk on wounded feet to the front door of my home. You may think me a cad, but by God, I'll show you I'm not because I can't stand the idea of you in pain. Now stop thrashing about like an angry polecat," he growled.

Milly slowly stilled and wound her arms around his neck as she fully gave in to him. She bit her bottom lip, muttering under her breath about him being ridiculous.

He carried her in silence for several minutes before she spoke again, her voice less prickly.

"You called me sweetheart. Were you just saying that, like you would with any woman? Or did you mean..." She trailed off, a blush staining her cheeks. Every time she nibbled her lip, he wanted to lay her down on the nearest flat surface and claim her. With kisses, with his hands, with his body. His cock twitched at the mental image and he blew out a breath, trying to regain control.

"A man ought to have a pet name for his wife," he said. *Especially when he was coming to care for her...*he silently added.

"Hmm..." She made a sound that was halfway between a hum and a sigh.

"You object to being called sweetheart?"

"Oh, no," she said, a look of feigned innocence warning him she had something up her sleeve.

They fell into silence again, but it was less charged with tension than before.

"I've never been to the Cotswolds before," Milly suddenly volunteered, and he glanced down at her in surprise. "It's very colorful. Pepperwirth Vale is very green, but we don't have hills and wildflowers like this."

"And what do you think?" He looked around at the countryside, the sights so familiar to him. To her it must seem foreign and so different from the flat emerald woods of Pepperwirth Vale. He thought of everything he would show her of the Cotswolds soon, the river valleys, the high wind hills, narrow paths, and lush shires. The chain of limestone hills slanting in a thin strip from northeast to southwest. This fairyland with its wildflowers and tiny cottages and Elizabethan era charm ran deep in his blood, as deep as the rivers that ran through the valleys. This place was a part of him, more than he could explain to his new wife. It would have been easy to sell his estate and walk away, but he couldn't sell a part of his heart. He wanted Milly to like it as much as he did. This was to be her home and he wanted her to be happy.

"It's lovely. More lovely than I expected."

Her reply pleased him so much that he was grinning by the time they finally reached the front gardens of Wesden Heath. The sun was hanging just above the horizon, casting a gold glow of evening light over the house and grounds.

"Let me down. I should walk to the door." She patted his chest gently and he stopped.

"Ready?" he asked. When she nodded, he carefully let her legs drop down and then let her go, but only enough to make sure she could stand.

"Well? What do you think of it?" He waved a hand at the gray stone manor house. Ivy climbed the walls at the base and wisteria laced the bay windows of the rooms facing the front of the house during the spring and summer months. A stone fountain with a rim covered in moss was in the center of the wild, unkempt gardens. A pang of sadness struck him. There was so much that he needed to repair on the property.

"It's..." Milly tilted her head as she studied the manor house. "It's beautiful, but it needs a lot of work, doesn't it?"

Owen cleared his throat. "Er...yes. Quite a bit." He rubbed the back of his neck. A jittery sense tingled through him as they approached the house. The front door opened and a matronly woman in a black dress rushed out.

"Master Hadley, we expected you so much sooner. Where is the car?"

"I'm sorry, Mrs. Nelson. The cab lost a tire and we were forced to walk the last seven miles."

The housekeeper covered her mouth. "Good heavens! Come inside at once. We will get you both settled."

"That would be good. Mrs. Nelson, this is my wife, Mildred; Mildred, this is the housekeeper, Mrs. Nelson."

"Welcome to Wesden Heath, Mrs. Hadley," the housekeeper said.

"Thank you. Did my maid, Constance, arrive yesterday?" Milly inquired as she followed Mrs. Nelson inside.

"Yes, she's all settled in," Mrs. Nelson said.

Owen trailed behind them as he entered the front door of the house. Mr. Boyd, the butler, rushed in the hall, his cheeks ruddy, his breath heavy.

"My apologies, Mr. Hadley. We weren't sure what time to expect you when you did not turn up this afternoon. I will have Cook prepare a meal for you and Mrs. Hadley."

"Very good, Boyd. Send it to my chamber and we shall dine there tonight."

"Of course, sir." Boyd then introduced himself to Milly before he ducked out of sight, heading for the kitchens.

"Milly, let me take you to your room and get you settled. We'll have a quick dinner upstairs tonight." Owen crooked his elbow out and she slid her arm through his.

As they walked up the stairs, he tried not to think about the state of the worn carpets and dusty bannisters. When Milly's gloved hand brushed against the wood, it came away with a smudge of grime. He had never been ashamed of his home before, but in that moment, he was.

The daughter of a viscount was used to something better than his. What could she think of him and Wesden?

The grounds and house were in need of so much care. If she didn't love Wesden, then she wouldn't be happy, and an unhappy Milly meant the shrewish temperament might return. It was not a prospect he looked forward to.

He paused in front of a bedroom, the one he'd directed to be prepared for her a week after their marriage plans had been announced in the banns. It was a few rooms away from his own chamber, which at the time had seemed not nearly far enough away. At first he'd been relieved that custom dictated a wife would have her own bedchamber. But now...now he wished they had connecting rooms, ones that made them feel more like man and wife.

People who shared their lives together usually came to care about each other. His parents had kept separate rooms and they had been able to avoid each other. He'd assumed he might face that possibility with Milly, but... not anymore. He wanted an intimate marriage, not just physically but emotionally. He'd never been one to live a lonely life and he wasn't about to start now. Owen had a sneaking suspicion that Milly might be amenable to it, too, if he could keep stealing kisses and find a way to melt the icy walls around her warm heart.

He wanted her to be close. It was a damnably foolish notion to crave her nearness, to ache to take her to bed, but he did. Even when she pushed him away, she fascinated him. Milly was a tightly wound bundle of contradictions that made little sense to him, and he had the strongest desire to spend the rest of his life untangling the mystery of who she really was. Temptress or shrew?

"These are your rooms. Your lady's maid should have her own chambers in the servants' hall. If either of you have need of anything, there are bells, of course. Mr. Boyd and Mrs. Nelson can see to anything you require." He opened the door to Milly's room. Constance was already inside, waiting patiently by the bed. Milly's shoulders relaxed visibly and she smiled for the first time in hours.

"Constance." The one word, so full of relief on her lips, made his chest ache. He rubbed at the spot with one hand but dropped it when she turned back around to face him.

"Thank you, Owen. I should like to have some time alone after our journey." She was glancing about the room, avoiding his gaze.

"Are you sure? I'd be happy to help you settle in," he offered. The thought of her pulling away from him after everything they had shared made him feel hollow. He didn't want to live with a stranger for the rest of his life. He'd rather have her spitting mad and railing at him for something thoughtless he'd said about her books than have her ignoring him.

"No, I'll be quite fine on my own. What time is dinner? Will there be a formal table prepared? Or should I expect something more casual?" Her tone was cool not cold, but it made him want to growl. This wasn't the Milly he'd wanted to see. This was the Milly from before they'd married, the cool socialite who walled her heart in ice. There was no hint of the intimacy that had been growing between them. They'd made progress this afternoon, and now she was attempting to move backward. He'd be damned if he let her shut him out again. He clenched his fists at his side. He would have to overwhelm her with passion, it was the only time he could break down that frosty wall she'd erected to keep him out. When Milly was kissing him, she wasn't cold or closed up; she was a different woman, a passionate, wild creature that smiled and laughed. A woman he could come to love with a little time. And that was what he wished for, to have a wife he could love, who might love him back.

"I'm not sure. I'll come to collect you. Since we will dine in my chamber, no need to dress up. Wear whatever you wish."

She nodded politely and tapped one booted foot, apparently more than ready for him to leave.

"Well...I'll see you in a short while," he said, and she promptly shut the door in his face.

"I'll see you in a short while." He sounded like an idiot. With a low growl, he stalked off toward his own chambers and slammed the door.

Chapter Eight

Milly sagged onto the four-poster bed, sinking into the soft mattress. Her feet stung and she was exhausted enough that she could have fallen asleep right there, if her stomach would stop grumbling.

"Milady?" Constance put a gentle hand on her forehead, as though testing her for a fever. "Are you well?"

With a heavy sigh, she responded, "Yes, well enough. Our cab ruptured a tire and we had to walk seven miles to get here."

Her maid winced and immediately reached for Milly's booted feet. "Shall I remove these for you?"

"Please," she almost begged, but it was so out of character for her that she didn't miss Constance's little smile. When the boots come off and she peeled her stockings down, she winced and hissed as she discovered blisters on her heels. A few places were rubbed bloody and raw.

"Oh!" Constance gasped.

Milly closed her eyes for a second, breathing. The cold air stung the wounded areas, but after a few seconds the burning eased.

"I'll fetch a healing balm. Whatever Mr. Evans can find." Constance left her alone and she curled up in a ball on the bed, pulling the counterpane over herself to stay warm. A small fire was in the hearth, but it didn't warm her up as much as she hoped it would.

I'll just rest until she gets back. Shouldn't be too long.

When she opened her eyes again, she found Constance peering down at her, worry knitting her brows together.

"Mr. Hadley is waiting for you to join him in his chambers for dinner." Constance held out slippers for her to put on and a thick woolen shawl to wrap around her shoulders.

Milly flinched as she eased her feet into the slippers but was relieved that she wouldn't have to put the boots on again. Then she tightened the shawl and squared her shoulders.

"Constance, what's the staffing situation like here? There should be more fires, less dust…less…" She rubbed her eyes with her thumb and forefinger before blowing out a breath.

Her lady's maid met her gaze steadily. "We need to hire

at least three footmen, four upstairs maids, and a scullery maid. As of right now, Wesden Heath has a butler, housekeeper, cook, one maid, and one footman." Constance ticked off the servants on her fingers as she paced back and forth in front of Milly. Milly bit her lip to hide her smile. Constance, even though she was a lady's maid, was more suited to the role of army general, or perhaps housekeeper. If Mrs. Nelson retired, Milly would have to see that Constance was offered the position.

"It is a good thing my father left me in some control of the finances. We can pursue the issue of the staff tomorrow morning."

"Very good, milady," Constance said.

"No more of that milady, Constance. I'm merely a gentleman's wife now," she reminded her maid gently.

Constance looked heavenward as though beseeching the angels to intercede before she turned to tidy the toilette items on the little vanity table, muttering, "You cannot take the blue blood out of a lady."

Milly checked her appearance in the tall looking glass and swept her hands over the messy style of her once-tidy coiffure. Sleeping without taking her hair down had been a little foolish, but she had been so exhausted she had no thought of it.

"Heavens, I look a fright," she said, and pinched her pale cheeks before heading to the door. She looked dreadful in her rumpled traveling clothes, slippers, and shawls, but after everything she had been through today, she was simply unable to care. Most gentlemen who married a lady of her standing would expect perfection in a wife every minute. Milly hoped Owen did not, because she was too exhausted to do anything about her appearance tonight, no matter how much she might wish to look her best out of habit.

She retraced her steps back down the hall to find the only other room on the upstairs floor that looked occupied. A sheen of gold light illuminated the bottom of the door, showing someone had a fire and lamps lit. She rapped her knuckles lightly and the door swung open a moment later.

"There you are. I was about to send out a search party." Owen stepped back, allowing her to brush past him to enter the room. He wore only trousers and a white shirt, the sleeves rolled up. His room was warm and welcoming with a healthy fire, unlike her chambers, which had been so cold her fingers were white and as brittle as icicles. She shivered and grasped the loose ends of her shawl as she headed straight for a chair by the fire.

"Cook made some spiced beef and soda bread for us," Owen said as he joined her. "I know you are used to more impressive fare, but I assure you I will send Mrs. Nelson to town tomorrow with a list of everything you desire."

Milly didn't look his way, even though she wanted to. If she looked at him and saw that handsome face turned to hers, she would cave in to her desire to get closer to him. The almost boyish hopefulness to his tone made her feel melancholy and a little fluttery inside. The strange mix of emotions was puzzling, but she reminded herself to keep her distance. She couldn't afford to fall in love with this man, no matter how sweet, charming, and completely seductive he could be. If she didn't protect her heart, he might leave her to slowly drown in a quiet life of desperation for loving a man who would never treat her as an equal. She'd seen it so many times before with other women her age who'd been born with a desire to be something more than simply a wife and mother.

"Thank you," she replied.

He walked away but returned a moment later with a cart and a tarnished silver tray with food. The aroma of the spiced beef made her stomach grumble. She could already taste the juniper and peppercorn spices that must have been soaked in the beef for a week. It was a simple meal, but a satisfying one. She selected a plate and cut a piece of brown soda bread and selected several slices of beef. Owen did the same and reached for a tall clear bottle filled with a pale cherry-red liquid.

"Care for some sloe gin?" He waved the bottle in invitation.

"Sloe gin?" She'd never heard of such a drink.

"Yes." His lips twitched. "It's made from the fruit of black thorn trees. It's a little sour but you harvest the fruit in early autumn." He poured her a small glass and she took it, studying it curiously.

"I've never had gin before." She grinned despite herself and took a sip. She gasped as the taste hit her hard.

Owen lunged for her, smacking a palm on her back as she coughed.

"Take it easy," he chuckled. "The next sip will go down easier, I promise." He nudged the glass in her hand with his fingertip.

She hesitated, eyeing the red liquid with more respect than curiosity as she took a sip again. It burned, but in a pleasant way now as it coated her tongue and throat. This time she tasted the tart fruit and a hint of sugar.

Owen leaned forward in his chair, his elbows resting on his knees as he watched her. The amused expression on his face softened his handsome features, and that little traitorous part of her that desired him beyond good sense and reason flared to life. The light-headedness from the gin didn't help either.

"This is very strong." She noted, then giggled.

Owen poured himself a glass and consumed it in one long gulp. "My family has been making sloe gin for generations. It's a tradition here, and helps keep us warm in the winter."

"Hmm." She took another sip and giggled again as the room spun slightly.

"Oh dear, you don't last long in your cups, do you?

Better eat something." He tilted his head at her plate and she ate heartily. The ache in her belly from hunger abated with each bite and she even did the most unladylike thing, licking the crumbs of soda bread from her fingers.

They dined in silence, with the crackle of the fire lulling Milly into a bit of warmth and comfort. She still felt off balance in her new surroundings, and she hated that. Control was paramount; control was safe. But she could control so little of what was happening now. She felt like the kitten she and her mother had once found caught outside in the gardens during a thunderstorm. They'd rescued it and brought it inside. Its tiny little body, shaking and wet, had clung to her skirts with its last bit of strength. She was clinging to Owen like that little cat, exhausted, terrified, and afraid to let go. It was a sad bit of irony that the very man who'd caused her to be in this situation was now the only person, aside from Constance, she felt safe with and on steady ground.

"Milly." Owen set his plate down and crossed his arms over his chest, his expression serious.

"Yes?" She curled her legs up under her on the chair but winced at the stab of pain from rubbing against her blisters.

"You're hurt?" He moved too fast, standing and towering over her in an instant as he bent to reach for her legs.

"I'm fine," she protested, trying to avoid his touch,

but he trapped her in the chair and she couldn't escape. He knelt in front of her, lifted her skirts, and examined her feet. When he removed one of the slippers, he tensed and raised his head to look up at her. His eyes were dark and warm, tinged with anger, too.

"Why didn't you say something sooner?"

She shrugged. "And have you carry me for seven miles? Don't be ridiculous."

He scrubbed a hand over his jaw and frowned, his lips parted as though he planned to speak but he clamped them shut, still scowling.

"What were you going to say?" she prodded.

He still held her one bare foot in his hand and he rubbed soothing small circles on the arch. She wiggled her toes when he still refused to answer.

"When I made plans for you to live here, I selected your chambers down the hall. I assumed that you would wish to have separate rooms away from mine. But I don't want that, not anymore." He resumed his caressing of her foot, then slid his hand to her ankle, shaping her bare calf.

"I don't understand." It was hard to formulate thoughts, let alone words when he was rubbing her very exposed skin.

"I would like for you to consider sharing my bed tonight. The room you're in now is in the cold part of the house, and until we've fixed up Wesden a bit, I'd much rather know you were warm and comfortable. *Here.* With me. If you decide you still don't like me after your rooms have been more fortified, you may move permanently into them. But for now, I'd like you to be with me."

Her breath caught in her throat and the gin made her feel...happy. She shouldn't want to sleep in his bed with him, not when she had vowed to keep herself distant.

"You won't argue with me, will you?" He shifted closer on his knees, raising her skirts to her lower thighs before he removed her second slipper and worked his magical fingertips along her other foot, massaging away the aches and pains. A fuzzy, warm feeling cloaked her and it wasn't just from the gin any longer.

"Not tonight." She leaned back in her chair and let him continue to rub her feet.

"Very well." His laugh was soft and rich, burning her inside like the gin.

Owen stood and with deft hands, swung her up into his arms and walked the few feet to the bed and set her down.

"Stay here while I find you a nightdress." He exited his chamber.

While he was gone, she unbound her hair and combed her fingers through the long strands, detangling small knots. Then she peeled back the covers of the bed and slipped beneath them. His bed was warm, and the fire heated the room much better than her chamber down the hall.

The walls of Owen's room were a buttery yellow with portraits of his ancestors hanging there. She saw a slight resemblance, mainly about the mouth and eyes. Owen's lips were seductive, full and soft. She'd studied them often enough over the last few days that they'd become a part of her waking fantasy. She leaned over the edge of the bed to see past the canopy hangings and took in the sight of the elegant plasterwork ceiling. Tree branches and vines with flowers created a forest above her head. Wesden Heath may be old and in much need of care, but what was here was elegant, beautiful. It would be easy to come to love this house as much as she did Pepperwirth Vale.

"You like it?" Owen's voice made her tense, then relax. He'd snuck back into the room without her noticing. A nightdress hung over one of his arms.

"It's beautiful," she agreed, nodding at the ceiling.

"It was inspired by the Vine Room at Kellie Castle." He walked around the bed to stand in front of her.

"I've been to Kellie Castle." She smiled. "I thought this looked familiar but couldn't quite place it." She looked up at him, feeling the height difference much more acutely because he stood over her while she sat upon his bed. A little shiver wracked her at the thought of being so much smaller than him. She hadn't thought she'd ever like feeling smaller, but with Owen, it didn't seem frightening; rather it felt exciting. Every time he was close to her and she felt the heat of his body and the size of him compared to her, it made her heart race and her breath catch in her throat.

"Would you like my assistance in helping you change?" He held up the nightdress.

"What?" Her voice came out high-pitched and breathless.

"Would you like me to help you out of those clothes?" His reply was low and soft as he grasped her hands and lifted her out of the bed to stand on her feet.

When she turned her back to him, he began unhooking the back of her navy skirt. The pressure of his hands was hot against her skin through the thin fabric of her blouse and chemise. Cold air kissed the backs of her legs as her skirt fell into a pool on the floor. Before she could turn or speak, his hands were coming around the front of her to unbutton her blouse. His body was so warm behind her that she couldn't resist the temptation to lean back against him as he parted her shirt. He gently pushed her forward a few inches so her shirt could slide off her body. A shiver wracked her as she stood there, wearing nothing but her chemise.

Practically naked. Her shoulders were bare since the chemise had slender lacy straps, rather than sleeves. Owen stroked one hand up her right arm to her shoulder, then across her collarbone and down to the valley of her breasts. Her breathing quickened and she panted softly as he pressed his hand above her heart.

"It's beating so fast," he whispered. The featherlight touch of his lips against the shell of her ear sent a bolt of heat to that secret spot between her thighs.

"Don't be frightened," he coaxed. "I would never hurt you." He curled one arm around her waist, keeping her pressed back against him. His other hand began to lift the edge of her chemise up, inch by inch. Her knees locked together, but he continued to glide his hand up her thigh, sliding his fingers over to fall between her legs. As he did, his mouth pressed lingering, soft kisses on her ear, her jaw, the nape of her neck. The delicate flick of his tongue in her ear was enough to make her gasp and jerk against him as her body hummed to life.

"That's it, sweetheart," he encouraged moments before his hand reached the juncture of her thighs. He cupped her mound, gently rubbing. His other hand on her waist moved up to grip her throat, and she arched her back. He seduced *ruthlessly*, his kisses perfectly placed on her throat to make her purr and moan. It was overwhelming, the feel of him possessively cupping her sex, putting pressure on an area she didn't know would respond with such a potent touch. When his teeth lightly raked her skin and he nipped her earlobe, she thought she was going to die with the building tension and pleasure. Wriggling her bottom against his groin, she tried to get him to do something, anything to ease the ache in her womb.

Owen parted the slick folds of her sex, exploring her

with one fingertip, the sensation so shocking she hissed out a breath.

"Owen, what are you doing?" she demanded, breathless and scandalized.

His rough chuckle against her neck made her belly quiver.

"I'm learning your body, sweetheart. What touches, what strokes, drive you to sweet madness."

Sweet madness? She was certain she was already there. His intimate touch would have made her blush and shy away from him if she hadn't already been flushed and caught in his embrace. They moved two steps forward, until the front of her knees and lower thighs hit the bed. He used his own body to trap her against the mattress.

"God, Milly," he groaned against her neck, and that ragged exhalation of her name sent her spiraling into a frightening, yet exciting place within herself she'd never experienced.

"How does it feel?" he asked, his finger drawing teasing patterns in the most sensitive part of her.

"Good..." She hesitated and then tensed and grasped his wrist, but didn't pull his hand away from between her thighs.

"Please don't tell me to stop." It was the closest thing she'd heard to begging from him.

Could she let him do this? Push her past a boundary of intimacy she'd never thought she'd give any man?

"Let me show you how good it can be." His fingers nudged her entrance and the strangled little sound of shock and his heavy breathing were the only sounds in the room besides the fire.

"Owen!" She clung to his arm that still held her by the throat, keeping her against him as he thrust one finger inside her. The feeling of that small penetration into her swollen channel made her instinctively clench around him. He rocked his hips against her from behind and the hard press of his arousal in the cleft of her buttocks built a new wave of heat inside her.

"Just tell me one little word, Milly. *Yes*. That's all I need to hear."

Chapter Nine

One word. Milly could tell Owen yes...*and he'd make love to me tonight.*

If she said yes, everything would change between them. She was scared of change, but she also knew that this was inevitable, not because he was her husband, but because she wanted to be with him.

To bloody hell with silly schoolgirl reservations. She was going to do it.

"Yes."

"Thank God." He spun her around in his arms and kissed her a second later. She heard the sound of fabric ripping and then her chemise fluttered to the ground in a heap of crumbled silk. She was completely naked.

"So beautiful. Do you know how beautiful you are?" Owen's rough voice made every part of her lower body burn. She attempted to cover her breasts, but he caught her wrists, holding them away from her body. Milly was afraid to look up at him, afraid to believe his words weren't true.

"Look at me, sweetheart." His voice was soft, coaxing, and she couldn't resist. When their gazes met, she held her breath, startled to see stark hunger and appreciation gleaming in his eyes. He really did think she was beautiful.

"I won't lie to you, ever," he vowed. "Now, lie back and let me enjoy you, wife." That flirtatious smile on his face was sharp with desire and a new flutter of nerves stirred in her belly.

"What about your clothes?" She sat on the edge of the bed, secretly delighting in the sinful sensation of her bare bottom on the sheets.

"What?" He chuckled, his gaze raking down her body, clearly not paying attention to what she'd asked him.

"Your clothes, husband. Off. Now." She pointed a finger at his chest, waving it up and down to indicate he shrug out of his clothes. "I'm not going to be the only naked person in this bed. We ought to be even." She waited, raising her chin in a way that would make her appear imperious and convey that she *must* be obeyed. But she had to bite her lip to hide a smile. It also helped to mask the shyness she was feeling of being completely bare and in his bed.

"Very well, you demanding little creature. She who

must be obeyed." He winked as he shrugged out of his shirt and unbuttoned his trousers.

He'd somehow removed his boots without her noticing earlier, which would make it easier for him to shuck off his trousers. That was the last barrier between them, she knew. Once he removed his pants, this thing would happen between them. Knowing that sent little tremors of excitement and anticipation through her.

When he started to tug his trousers down, Milly was distracted by the fascinating V-shaped muscles of his lower belly that carved an obvious path down to his groin. His hands paused and she glanced up at his face to find him watching her.

"Have you ever seen a man..." He shook his head. "No, of course you haven't."

"Seen what? A naked man?" It was easy enough to gucss his thoughts.

"You haven't, have you?" His eyes narrowed slightly in mild suspicion.

This time she smiled. "Of course I have." She leaned back on the bed, propping herself up on the pillow like a sultana.

His dark eyes lingered on the tips of her breasts, the way her small nipples pebbled in the cold air. She sensed he was figuring out her secret, that she'd never seen a living man naked.

"You are too cunning, wife. I believe you have seen statues, but no men of flesh and blood."

With a final knowing glance at her, he dropped his trousers and smallclothes, stepping out of the mess of fabric to stand proudly at the foot of the bed, a grin raking over his suddenly wolfish features. Her curious gaze dropped to his groin and she tensed, every bone and muscle inside her clenching painfully together. The man would have shamed a stallion.

"That"—she cleared her throat—"that will not fit. You're far too large."

Again, he laughed, the rich sound only upsetting her this time.

"What's so amusing?" she demanded. He walked to the side of the bed, nearest her.

He cupped her chin and met her gaze. "It will fit. It will likely hurt a little at first, but you will stretch to accommodate me. I will do my best to ease the initial pain." Bending over, he brushed a kiss over her lips and then indicated that she scoot over on the bed to allow him to lie beside her.

"Why don't we get under the covers," he suggested.

Milly swallowed hard and nodded, pulling the covers up to her waist as she moved back to give him room. He joined her and before she had the chance to think twice or change her mind, he curled his body around hers, kissing her. The friction of her breasts rubbing against his chest and his left thigh nudging hers apart was exotic, strange, and left her breathless with a whisper of a thrill. His hands stroked her, tracing her hip and cupping her buttocks. He clenched one globe, the hard grasp creating a delicious tingle within her. Sparks flared in the little bundle of nerves and deep within her abdomen. His erection bobbed against her stomach and she curled her fingers around it, squeezing lightly. She was still a little frightened at his size, but she was too aroused to resist the urge to touch him. Owen hissed and rocked his hips.

"Christ, woman, you know how to set a man aflame." His throaty, half-laughing response made her smile nervously back at him.

"Am I doing something wrong?" She started to let go, but his hand came down over hers, keeping her fingers around his shaft.

"Stroke me, love, slow and gentle, and I'll stroke you." He slid his hand between her thighs and penetrated her with a finger, probing, then thrusting. Milly had to concentrate on touching him back, but it was so difficult when his finger inside her made her want to squirm, to arch her back, to claw at him for something else she wasn't sure she could handle.

"Owen, I feel a little strange," she breathed in between kisses. He smiled against her mouth, continuing to rub a spot inside her that made her jerk and made pleasure/pain zing straight to her breasts.

"Strange how?" he asked.

"Heavy and yet fluttery inside at the same time. Is that possible?"

He feathered a kiss across her lips before withdrawing his hand.

"Lie on your back, sweetheart." He helped her to lie flat and she tensed when he nudged her knees apart.

"Trust me, Milly. Trust me." He caged her beneath him, settling his hips between her thighs. She stiffened, terrified of what would happen next.

"Breathe with me." He dropped his head to kiss her again and when nothing happened, she relaxed and surrendered to the pleasure of his kiss. She wasn't sure how long their mouths moved in harmony, but suddenly between one breath and the next, he had positioned his shaft at her entrance and thrust into her. The unexpected pressure and the stinging pain left her breathless. He moved out a little and she bit her lip, shutting her eyes.

Breathe through the pain. She dug her nails into Owen's shoulders.

"Most of the pain is over," he murmured, true apology in his eyes. "Just breathe and relax. After that there will be only pleasure." He kissed her chin, then moved his lips down to her collarbone, then to her left breast. He nuzzled the peak and then sucked the nipple into his mouth. Milly moaned at the pleasurable delight of his mouth nibbling on so sensitive a part of her.

One of his hands palmed her knee, moving up and down her outer thigh in soothing strokes. When he rocked forward again, the pain was more of a ghost than real, and a few seconds later she realized there was only a wild sense of need, that building pressure and ache that Owen's body was satisfying. Each time he pumped into her, their pelvises touched and they were as close and connected as two beings could be.

After that, she didn't need words, nor did he. He captured her wrists on either side of her head, pinning them into the bedding. It left her helpless but excited as he thrust into her, harder, until she was on the edge, the force making them both gasp and share soft cries. Milly realized she liked the roughness, the way he claimed her, *consumed* her. Their eyes were locked; nothing else outside them existed. Nothing but their shared breaths, the point of connection between them and the ecstasy of his body atop hers. Everything in her splintered in bursts of endless pleasure. A cry left her lips and it merged with Owen's hoarse shout of her name. *Milly*. She smiled, gasped for breath, and went utterly limp. Owen's weight settled more firmly on top of her.

"Are you all right?" he asked between his own ragged breaths, his hands still gripping her wrists, keeping her trapped, but she didn't mind.

"Y-yes." She kept smiling and he grinned down at her.

"Good. I was a little overeager and was afraid I'd been

too rough." He withdrew from her body, released her hands, and rolled off her. The instant loss of his body and heat, their connection, impacted her more than she wanted it to.

"Is this the part where men usually leave their wives alone?" she asked, feeling very small and insignificant. She glanced down and played with a loose lock of her hair.

Owen tipped her chin up and brushed the backs of his knuckles over her cheek, a tender smile flirting with his lips, as though he sensed her insecurity.

"Usually, but not me. Why do you think I brought you to *my* bed? I'm not going anywhere." He traced her lips with a fingertip, then kissed her thoroughly. That wonderful warmth spread through her all over again from just his kiss.

"Get some sleep. Tomorrow we have much to do." He tucked her body against his and she let him, loving the way he held her so close. He was the one comforting, familiar thing in the strange new world that was to be her home. She could let him hold her for one night. Surely it wouldn't risk her heart, not one night...

Owen held on to Milly, counting her dark eyelashes and humming inside with pleasure as she surrendered to sleep in his arms and his bed. To woo a woman was easy, but to woo one's own wife? That was another feat entirely. She was too skittish, ready to bolt at the first hint of being hurt. That was the last thing on earth he wished to do to her.

She'd gotten hurt tonight. Losing her virginity hadn't been painless, but she'd gotten through it, the poor girl. Now she was on the other side, a woman who'd tasted pleasure in a man's arms.

I just have to convince her to trust me. He'd known from the start she saw him as a ruthless fortune hunter bent only on taking a woman's money. But that wasn't who he was, not deep down, and he needed her to know the real him because if she did...she might come to love him, and that mattered. Life had forced him to marry for money but that's not what he had truly ever wanted for himself. He didn't want a loveless marriage like his parents had.

She burrowed closer, clinging to him, pressing her cheek against his shoulder. The feel of her lying skin to skin with him was oddly harmonious, like a chord on a pianoforte. Different, yet when blended together, it felt right.

"I want to keep you, Milly," he whispered softly enough that she didn't stir. "And what a challenge that will be, eh?" He knew enough of her now to realize tonight was only a small victory in the battle to win her. Milly was infinitely complex. Unbelievable lovemaking would not be enough to tame her or ease her fears of rejection or mockery. To woo her, he would need to be careful, considerate, kind, and yet never allow her to gain an inch in the battle that lay between them. If this was to be a happy marriage, he would have to get his wife to fall in love with him. A month ago, he would have laughed at the impossible task and walked away, but he couldn't do that. Not after the promise he made to her father and the promise he made to himself.

There will be happiness in this marriage.

He tugged the blankets up around them and let sleep claim him. But the dreams were never far behind. The dreams of darker days and hellish nights during the war. Such things were always running just beneath the surface of his mind and in the corners of his heart.

He'd only just closed his eyes when old memories surged up around him. Choking him.

The blazing sun scorched his skin, the buzz of flies around the bodies, carrion birds hopping among the corpses, picking at decaying flesh. His own hands stained with blood, too slick to maintain the hold of his rifle. He clawed his way through the African underbrush, unable to see his troops. There was only blood and death...and silence. That was the worst part after a battle. When the crack of guns and boom of cannons had died and the fog of war had been blown away by the breeze...silence was all that was left. Owen tried to fight off the rising panic. His men had left him behind to die. He would die. A few more hours with no water, no food, no shelter from a merciless sun.

"God forgive me for my sins," he muttered, his voice hoarse.

Something jostled his shoulder and he jerked up violently, finding himself back in the dark firelight bedchamber of Wesden Heath. Not Africa. The war was over. His hands were clean. He lifted his palms up, studying them in the dim light.

"What's the matter?" Milly asked. "You were thrashing about in your sleep. Are you all right?"

He braced his arms on his raised knees as he caught his breath. His lungs were still burning as though he'd been struggling for air.

"It's the—" He paused, realizing he'd been about to confess his deepest shame. He'd told her once before about the dreams, but he hadn't told her how deeply they affected him. How he feared closing his eyes sometimes at night because he was terrified of what he would see. A man shouldn't admit to fear, especially not to a woman. She would think he was incapable of protecting her.

"What?" she pressed.

"Just a dream," he finally said. "I'm sorry I woke you."

"Just a dream?" Milly echoed. "It was a nightmare about the war, wasn't it?"

He couldn't answer that; the admission would be too much of a weakness.

An elegant hand settled on his shoulder, the touch sweet and comforting. When had any woman ever treated him like this? A touch that wasn't meant to entice or seduce. It made him hungry for her even more, just thinking about the kind heart she kept hidden from the world beneath her tough exterior.

I'm beginning to understand you, wife. He almost smiled. Almost. Instead he covered her hand with his, giving it a gentle squeeze before he let go.

"You should try to sleep." She stroked his hair out of his eyes and he sighed at the way it felt.

"There can't be any more nightmares," she whispered close to his ear. "Not when you come home. This is a safe place, your own room, your own bed." She surprised him by placing a kiss on his cheek and then she pulled him back down in his bed beside her, curling her body around his.

He did feel safe. As though her words had cast a spell over him, one of peace and trust.

I'm home. Not in Africa. The war is over. I'm home. When he pulled the blankets back up, he rolled to face Milly. Her eyelids had fallen to half-mast and she put a fist over her mouth to stifle a little yawn.

Was she afraid to be here? In a strange land, in a strange bed, with a stranger? The woman was so brave, and she was only doing her duty, as many hundreds of thousands of women had done before. How foolish he'd been to think women knew nothing of suffering or fear or sacrifice. And Milly hadn't had to say a word to show him where her strength lay.

"I'm so sorry I woke you." He found himself apologizing again.

"Don't apologize," she murmured sleepily. "I'm glad I could offer some comfort as you have done for me."

A thousand words rested on the tip of his tongue, but he had no bravery of his own to say them. Instead, he cupped her chin and lifted her face up to press a lingering kiss on her lips, savoring this quiet moment just between the two of them. Tomorrow would come soon enough and with it, another battle to win her heart.

Chapter Ten

"Are you trying to kill me, woman?" Owen's harsh growl turned into a violent cough as a massive wave of dust swept across the room straight toward him. He blinked through bleary eyes at his wife. She was tugging a thick green baize curtain away from the tall windows of the library. Morning sunlight shot through the room, hitting the tall shelves and the rows of endless books. Motes of dust danced through the beams in the wake of Milly flinging curtains back.

"I'm not trying to kill you. Don't be so dramatic," Milly muttered as she hauled back a large wicker rug beater and smacked the curtain. Another cloud of dust erupted around them. Milly didn't cough. Owen stared at her. How the hell did she not cough? Then he realized her face was turning slightly red.

"Best not to forget to breathe, sweetheart," he added from a safe distance across the room because the glare she shot him assured him he would get swatted by the carpet beater if he was closer.

She stepped back from the curtain and sighed. "Are you going to stand there or are you going to help me?"

"I—"

"And answer carefully, husband, because I will not be beating these curtains by myself." She swung the wicker handle as effectively as a master fencer would his foil.

Suddenly Owen burst out laughing. There was something utterly delightful in his beautiful wife wielding a carpet beater and threatening him while looking divine in little black boots; a full, dark blue silk skirt; and a white blouse. Her hair was catching the sunlight just right, the dust settling on the crown of her hair glinting like diamonds. Owen's breath caught at the mixture of her glorious ferocity and beauty. *She who must be obeyed...*

"What is so funny?" She smacked the curtain again before rounding on him. He dodged around the nearest reading table, careful to stay back in case she swung it at him.

"You're so fetching when you're angry with me. Did you know that?" he teased, a wicked grin curving his lips.

"Fetching? Owen, blast it! We've been cleaning this house for the last week and you're thinking about how I look?"

It was true. He was completely guilty of thinking of her and getting her back into bed. For the last seven days they had been working themselves to exhaustion each night, cleaning every inch of the house and putting it to rights, but they'd only done half the work and they hadn't even started on the gardens. He usually prided himself on stamina but when they collapsed into bed, they went straight to sleep and it wasn't until each following morning when he'd been able to take his time and make love to her. Milly climaxing beneath him in early morning sunlight was truly a thing of beauty. Of course the moment they started cleaning, he couldn't help but quarrel with her, albeit with a small amount of amusement when they disagreed on almost everything. But, as he was happy to note, they were *learning* to talk to each other and figure out a mutual path, like partners rather than adversaries.

"Milly, sweetheart, I fully admit that thinking about getting you flat on your back is thc only thing that has crossed my mind since we left bed this morning."

A lock of hair escaped her elegant coiffure and fell into her eyes. She tilted her head slightly, her gaze softening.

"Really?" she whispered.

He sensed there was a danger to this answer, as though if he said sex was the only thing he thought about, it would upset her, but he knew that women also wanted to know they were desired. Deciding to brave his little harpy's wrath, he walked around the table to gently take the beater from her. After it was deposited on the reading table, he cupped her face in his hands and leaned in to press a feathery kiss to her lips before speaking. He smiled when her lashes fluttered closed for a brief instant as she lost herself to his kiss.

"My point is, you are all I think about, in bed and out. I haven't had this much fun in ages; tearing through the house with you and spending time with you has been wonderful."

Her striking blue eyes widened and her lips parted. "You're not just saying that? I thought I might have bored you when we were talking over supper last night."

"Bored me? Heavens no, I loved hearing you talk."

He'd listened to her talk for almost an hour about her dreams, about how she longed to teach underprivileged children, especially girls, to read. It had shocked him at first, to hear that a highborn woman of her pedigree would be interested in stooping to teaching village children, but then when he thought about it and her more closely, he realized he was understanding her better and better. She wanted freedom, she wanted a life outside of being a wife, and he couldn't fault her for that. But she always wanted to give that freedom to other girls. Increasing literacy would certainly give those young children a chance to grow up and live better lives than their parents had. If someone had tried to clip his wings, he would have felt suffocated and he didn't wish that fate upon anyone, especially not his wife.

"I thoroughly enjoyed listening to you. You are free to always talk to me about *anything.*"

She lowered her lashes and curled her fingers around his wrists as he still held her face in his hands. A blush stained her cheeks and she smiled. It was a warm smile, not a coy or cold one and it made his heart leap.

I might stand a chance to win her after all...

"Why don't we leave the curtains for another day? I think we deserve a bit of a reprieve, don't you?" He kissed the tip of her nose.

"That would be nice," she replied. Unable to still the excited beat of his heart, he curled an arm around her waist and escorted her from the library. Tonight, before dinner, he could return and collect a few books for her to read. He might just read them with her. For the first time in ages, Owen was struck by a sense of hope. Everything might yet turn out all right.

I may have muddled the beginning but I believe things are finally going well.

"GOOD HEAVENS, HE IS A SHAGGY LITTLE fellow, isn't he?" Milly stayed a step or two behind Owen as they approached the plump, wooly coated sheep.

They'd abandoned the library and the dusty curtains in favor of a walk outside for rest and fresh air.

"He's a fine example of the Cotswold lion." Owen waved her to step closer.

The sheep continued to munch on the plot of greenish brown grass about ten feet away.

"And how many of these lions do you have roaming about the estate?" Milly tucked her scarf around her neck and dared to come closer.

"We have close to a hundred here on Wesden property, and the tenant farmers on the surrounding lands have their own smaller flocks. It will likely grow in spring if the breeding is successful." Owen turned back to her and walked over, offering the crook of his elbow to her. He'd shown her much of the house already in the last week while they were cleaning and she'd begun an official list of everything she found fault with that would need to be addressed. The house needed more servants, food in its larders, and the rooms redecorated. The list was endless.

But she'd been surprised that he did in fact help her. She had expected him to leave her alone after their first night in bed and run off to London to escape the back-breaking work of fixing Wesden Heath. Yet he'd stayed... For an entire week they had worked together, side by side, often fighting, but eventually coming to an agreement and fixing whatever they were trying to repair.

Being around Owen was no longer a chore, nor did it

make her nervous. She was feeling more relaxed and more herself than she had in a long time. And in the morning… when he made love to her, it left her giddy and blushing like a schoolgirl but she couldn't help it. Part of her was afraid to trust this growing affection she had for him, but she also knew it was inevitable—she was going to fall in love with her husband. She buried the fear of losing her freedom and control of her life each time he smiled at her and kissed her.

"We could go into town if you like. The ride is quite pleasant."

He didn't own a car—only hired one when he needed it—but Milly knew they could certainly afford one now; she'd have to find a clever way of convincing him of this. Despite his need for her money, she sensed he was a bit of a slim spender.

"I'd like that. It has been ages since I've been on a horse."

She and Owen walked back across the fields, reaching a waist-high stone wall. He easily hopped the wall and then reached back over to pick her up by the waist, carrying her across the fence and then setting her down. All of the practical skirts she'd packed were most useful. Sadly, she guessed her lovely gowns for evening balls would rarely be worn. Such a pity, she did so love balls, even though she'd had no real chance to enjoy them. Avoiding suitors had been necessary but it had deprived her of the joys of dancing, laughing, being herself.

"What are you thinking about?" Owen asked as they entered the gardens in front of the house.

She answered honestly. "Dancing. I miss dancing."

His bark of laughter made her bristle.

"You could have fooled me. I distinctly recall you telling Hampton off when he asked you to dance."

Milly huffed, pulling her arm free of his as she stalked ahead of him.

"Oh no, you don't," Owen called out. His arms banded around her waist as he caught hold of her from behind.

She squealed in surprise and swatted at his hands but he twirled her around, lifting her enough that her boots skimmed the grass.

"Put me down, Owen. Heavens!" She squealed again as he set her on the ground, then spun her in his arms so that she faced him. The delighted and all-too-smug expression on his face made her want to smack his chest. So she did, but not too hard.

"Why not dance with me?" he suggested.

"What?"

He still held her waist, his grip firm but gentle.

"Dance with me, Milly. Come on."

It was impossible to deny Owen when he flashed that

smile of his. The one that made her chest ache and her knees wobbly.

"You like to dance, too?" she asked.

"More than anything," he replied, then seemed to reconsider. "Well, *almost* anything." He waggled his eyebrows at her.

"You mean...oh!" She felt the red-hot blush flood her entire body.

"Yes, what we did last night is much better than dancing." He kept one palm on her waist, the other clasping one of her free hands.

"A waltz?" he offered.

She could only shake her head. "This is ridiculous. We are in the middle of a country garden, not in a London ballroom."

"And that is exactly why we must dance."

"But we have no music." She desperately tried to find other excuses. If she danced with him...Her heart thumped wildly at the mere thought of how wonderful it might be.

Owen started to sing, just vocalizing a familiar waltz. His voice was beautiful. Lulled into the spell of his singing and the pull of his arms, they began to dance. The world around them spun in a shimmering haze as they twirled and whirled. The gravel of the garden path crunched beneath their boots and the occasional thrush chirped along with Owen's captivating melody. He was a wonderful dancer, anticipating her own pattern of steps as though they'd danced together for a hundred years. By the time he finally slowed their steps to a stop, she was humming along with him.

"There now, see? Breaking the rules of propriety can be fun."

She smiled. She supposed dancing in a garden wasn't exactly breaking propriety, but she hadn't thought she would ever do such a thing. He was right, though; it had been fun.

"Now, let's get to town. I peeked at your list this morning and we have quite a bit to accomplish."

Two hours later, she and Owen were visiting the last shop, a tiny bookseller, at Owen's request. Not that Milly would have argued, since she adored books. Owen didn't hover over her as she perused the shelves. The store didn't have many of the most current titles but that was no surprise. A small shop, out of the way of London, wasn't likely to have the latest books. She selected a few classic titles like *Ivanhoe* and *Emma* before she went in search of her husband. He was standing by the doorway of the shop, deep in conversation with another man.

Something about their rigid stances made her stay concealed, peering at them from around one of the bookshelves.

"Never thought I'd see you settle down, Hadley. Finally found a rich widow who doesn't mind paying your debts?" The barbed comment came from the other man and Owen clenched his hands into fists at his sides.

"Brandon, you are on dangerous ground." Owen's tone was low but hard as iron.

Brandon laughed.

"You went too far when you had an understanding with my sister. When you cried off, it broke her. She's never been the same, especially not after the scandal with her condition." Brandon growled. "No man would have her, even though the babe died." The last was uttered in a vicious growl.

Owen stepped back, his face ashen. Milly covered her mouth, hoping to quiet her frantic breathing.

A baby? He cried off an engagement and left a woman with child?

"It wasn't my child, Brandon. I broke it off because she didn't love me. She told me she loved someone else. I let her go. Whoever she was seeing put her in the family way, *not I*." The barely restrained fury sparked in Owen's eyes, so strong that Milly could see it from where she stood.

Brandon squared his shoulders, sneering. "My sister wouldn't lie. She said it was you."

Owen showed his teeth like a cornered wolf.

"I'm not going to be a scapegoat for Scarlett. I never bedded her. Do not put that lie on my doorstep."

Brandon stepped back, but his voice was icy. "I hope

your new wife learns what sort of man you are so she doesn't end up with child and alone." Then he stormed around Owen and exited the bookshop. Milly tried to duck behind the bookcase, but Owen glanced around and caught sight of her. The emotions racing across his features were wiped clean and he met her stare with a cold, blank expression.

"Milly, have you found any books you like?" he asked.

She was still clutching *Ivanhoe* and *Emma* to her chest. She nodded mutely and walked past him to the small shopkeeper's desk to pay for the books. Owen lingered by the doorway, restlessly pacing. Once she paid for her items, she tucked them in a small satchel and followed Owen out of the shop. Neither of them spoke on the ride back to Wesden Heath. Milly couldn't get the words out of her head.

Scarlett. A child...

When they reached the house, she was so numb inside that she didn't flinch when he helped her down from her horse.

"Milly," he began, then paused when she refused to meet his gaze.

"I think I'll take some tea in my chambers." She skirted around him and rushed to the house.

"Mistress," Mrs. Nelson greeted, but Milly fled past her, up the stairs to her room.

"Milady?" Constance leapt up from the seat by the fire, a pair of boots and a polish cloth in her hands.

"Oh, please sit, Constance," she all but gasped out. Why did she feel like she was going to cry? She shouldn't, but the tears were there, ready to fall. She would never forget what she'd overheard, that Owen was the seducer she'd always feared he was. A coldhearted man who took what he wanted and left devastation behind him. *This is why I refuse to fall in love. I'm not in love with him. I'm not.* Then why did it hurt so much? Why did the thought of him getting another woman with child feel like a knife to her heart? He'd seduced that woman just like he had seduced her and he'd abandoned that woman...just as he would abandon her. It was too much to bear, her heart shattering into a thousand glittering shards.

The door to her room crashed open as Owen strode in, a thunderous expression on his face.

"Excuse us, Constance." He cleared his throat and jerked his head toward the door.

"No, Constance, stay," Milly begged. Her poor maid looked between the two of them.

Owen crossed his arms over his chest.

"I won't bother you much longer, Milly, but we *will* talk."

Constance bolted for the door and left them completely and utterly alone. Owen closed the door and leaned back against it, preventing any means of escaping him.

"Owen, I have no interest in talking to you." She sat down in a chair by the fire and opened her satchel of books, pulling one out, not that she could actually read at a time like this.

Owen took the second chair by the fire and leaned forward, angling her chair toward his. He snatched the book and her satchel out of her hands, tossing them onto the bed.

"Listen to me. What you witnessed today doesn't have anything to do with what lies between us."

That lit a fury inside her to match his. "It clearly has nothing to do with us. You loved another woman, got her with child, then cried off. Thank heavens you never dared to love me. I should hate to think how I would have fared being a woman in such esteem in your affections."

Owen's eyes narrowed to dangerous slits.

"Scarlett was a woman I once cared deeply for. But I never loved her. Would I have married her? Yes. But she didn't love me. There was a young man who came through the village that summer, and she set her cap for him. She threw me over for the other man, and I let her. There was no reason to keep a woman trapped when she did not love me."

Milly almost scoffed. It wasn't as though he could have set her free; they were past the point of no return.

"We never made love. Not once. We shared a kiss or two, but I swear to you, Milly, it was not my child she bore and lost." His voice dropped and turned rough. "I swear to you on this house, on these lands that give me a reason to draw breath, that is the honest truth."

Her throat was squeezed so tight, she couldn't get a breath into her lungs for several long seconds. She wanted to cry. She wanted to scream, to hit him, to show him the pain that was tearing her up inside. Even if what he said was true, she was already cut and bleeding.

He stood, his lips parted as though to speak, when an urgent knock came at the door.

"Enter," he said.

Mr. Boyd came in, holding a piece of paper. "Telegram for you, sir. It was delivered just now from town. Urgent."

Owen didn't immediately take the telegram. He continued to watch Milly for a long moment before he accepted the slip of paper. When he unfolded it and read the words, he growled and crushed the paper in his palm before striding over to the fire and tossing it in the flames.

"I have to go to London tonight. I'll hire a cab from town and leave as soon as it arrives."

Milly swallowed the lump in her throat and looked at him. Stark pain laced his features and her bleeding heart quivered in response.

"I shall write to you. Every day. Please at least do me

the courtesy of reading my letters." His shoulders slumped and he exited the room.

She glanced back at the fire and noticed the telegram had fallen short of the flames. It rested on gray ashes, unburned. She used a poker to extricate the slip of paper and smothered it flat on the ground so she could read the message.

Jack drinking again. Need you to come at once. Only you can stop him. Hampton.

Jack? Was this Jack Watson, Owen's friend that went to war with him? Milly stared into the fire for a long while, the bit of the note still grasped in her hands. Who was Owen really? The rakish man who seduced women and left them in a state of trouble? Or was he a good man who dropped everything to help a friend? She wasn't sure what to think and she could only pray what she hoped in her heart was true. That Owen was the man she'd started to fall in love with. Her heart gave a shuddering few beats out of sync and she tried to catch her breath.

Please don't deceive me, Owen. Be that man I so wish you to be...

Her bedroom door opened and Constance entered, her eyes wide with worry.

"Milady? Is everything all right?"

Milly summoned up her courage and put on a brave face. "Yes. I should like to retire now."

She let Constance help her undress and then she

crawled under the covers, shivering from more than just the cold. She missed Owen's warm bed, but she missed Owen even more. A hundred thoughts fluttered through her mind and she couldn't sort any of them out.

It was going to be a long, cold, sleepless night.

Chapter Eleven

Owen felt like hell and knew he must have looked even worse when Leo's eyes widened at the sight of him. They were outside a rather awful little hovel of a place near White Chapel.

"I'm glad you arrived so quickly, but..." Leo brushed blond hair out of his eyes. "Is Milly making married life difficult?" He worded the question carefully.

"I don't want to talk about it. Where the bloody hell is Jack?" Owen brushed the travel dust off his sleeves and stared coldly at the pub house's wooden door. It was a nameless little hole in the wall, in utter shambles.

"He's inside. He refused to come out when I asked him to. He asked for you." Leo's eyes were heavy with sorrow.

"Very well, let's fetch him." Owen shouldered his way

into the dingy little pub and found Jack at once. He was slumped over a bar, his eyes glassy, an empty bottle loosely held in one hand, humming an old tune. At first the notes weren't recognizable, and off-key. Then Jack straightened a little and put more gusto into the sound and the tune changed, becoming a song Owen remembered. A song etched into his bones. It was a tune they'd sung during their days in Africa. A tune that froze Owen in his tracks for a few seconds. It was "*Goodbye, Dolly Gray,*" a song he and Jack had sung the night before half of their regiment had perished.

Blinding sun, decaying flesh, the cries of vultures, and the silence.

I can do this. He reminded himself the war was over, that he wasn't stranded in a foreign country surrounded by blood and death, not anymore.

"Jack," he said, his tone gentle but firm as he approached his friend. It had been months since he'd seen Jack Watson, and the days had not been kind to him. He was too thin, his cheeks too hollow, his once-muscled body weak from lack of food and exercise. At the sound of Owen's voice, Jack lifted his head, his eyes clearing a bit.

"Hadley," he sighed, and smiled. "Hampton said you'd come. I wanted to wait for you." His speech was thick with drink.

"And here I am. Why don't you take supper with Hampton and me?" Owen leaned against the bar, blocking some rows of liquor bottles from Jack's view. The pub was empty except for an ancient man at the far end of the bar, wiping pint glasses with a gray rag.

"Come on, Jack. Supper would be nice, wouldn't it?" Leo shared a worried glance with Owen; then when Jack turned to him, fire in his eyes, Leo backed up a step.

Owen hated this. He, Jack, and Leo had been friends —great friends—so long ago. Three mischievous lads at Eton sneaking out at night to get into mischief the way only boys could. They'd gone to Cambridge together, too, their bonds even tighter than before. But the war had eaten away at their boyhood ties. Leo had tended to his estate, while Jack and Owen had rushed off to Africa to fight the Boers. None of them could have known what awaited them on the shores of Africa—and even Jack, who had once been optimistic and carefree, was reduced to this most basic of beings. Jack had been unable to sleep, to eat; he curled up inside a bottle, ready to die. Leo had become the enemy to Jack, because he hadn't served; he couldn't understand the horrors, the sacrifices, the tragedy of war. Only Owen had held the three of them together by a grasp as tenuous as a fine thread.

"Jack, what if you come to Wesden Heath and spend some time with me?" Owen offered. As it was, it couldn't make things worse. Milly had run from him. She'd gotten hurt and withdrawn, just as he'd feared she would. He had no damned clue how to convince her he wasn't a blaggard.

If only he hadn't run into William Brandon, the damned ignorant fool. He'd told Milly the truth about Scarlett but it hadn't seemed to matter. The damage was done. She thought the worst of him. Spending some time with Jack couldn't be nearly as bad as being so close to his wife and having no way to touch her or hold her. She needed a reprieve from him to settle and he needed time enough to figure out how to win her back and return his home to the peace and comfort he'd been working toward.

"Come with you?" Jack blinked through bleary eyes.

"Yes. To Wesden Heath. It would do you good to spend time in the country." Owen shared a look with Leo and the other man gave a subtle nod.

"I suppose," Jack grumbled, and tried to stand. He made it two feet before the glass bottle he held slipped from his lax grip, shattering on the floor even as Leo and Owen swept in and grabbed Jack around the arms, supporting his dead weight.

"Do you need a cab back to Wesden?" Leo asked.

"No, I have one waiting for me at the corner. I'll bring him back to Wesden after he's had a week or so to sleep off the drink at a hotel," Owen explained. It would be easier to let Jack dry up in a hotel with Owen to watch over him and then bring him home to Wesden Heath, where he would have an easier chance of stealing liquor from cabinets and hiding it away for later consumption. If Owen could keep Jack confined in a small room without access to anything but food and water, he might be able to get him through the worst of his withdrawal.

"I'll be in London for a few days if you need me," Leo replied as they walked out of the pub and headed toward the hired cab waiting on the corner.

"Thank you," Owen said as he helped Jack into the back of the cab.

Leo took the front seat of the cab. "I'll ride with you and help you get him settled."

Owen nodded. The driver started the engine and headed for the hotel address Owen gave him. Owen vowed that the moment he reached the hotel, he'd write Milly a letter letting her know he was staying in town to help Jack. She deserved to *know* him, to understand his life, his past. Maybe she would be able to forgive him for having a past. None of it influenced his life now with her, but he had to make her understand that. He wanted their marriage to be a good one. Passion and love may someday be able to follow. He hoped.

She deserves to be loved, loved fiercely and passionately. And I want to be the man who loves her...

Milly collapsed into a plush chair in the library. A dinner tray sat on a nearby table. Mrs. Nelson had asked the cook to prepare another hearty feast of beef and soup, and Milly wondered if the woman was trying to fatten her up. She'd spent the entire day working alongside the new fleet of footmen and housemaids to train them and to determine what repairs and cleaning were needed on the rooms. Despite the new staff being able to take over the cleaning, she had worked alongside them, unable to sit still. If she did, she thought of Owen and it made her chest ache. Working herself to the bone had been the only way to dull the pain in her chest, and Wesden Heath looked much better for it. Old ratty drapes in three of the bedrooms had been removed and new fabrics ordered, carpets had been taken outside and beaten of their dust, and then the wood floors had been mopped and polished.

Mr. Boyd and Mrs. Nelson had balked at first when Milly had made it clear she wished to actually do much of the physical labor alongside the staff. They hadn't minded when Owen was there to join her, but now that there was plenty of help to go around, the servants had insisted she go rest. A few heated arguments had ensued throughout the morning following Owen's departure, but once the new staff had arrived, both the butler and the housekeeper were too distracted by the necessary training of the new young men and ladies to put up any resistance to Milly's new control of the house. After two days, everyone had settled into a routine of work while they waited for Owen to return.

Milly was exhausted after the last few days of hard

work and looked forward to a quiet evening reading in a chair with a blanket wrapped around her.

The library door opened and Mr. Boyd entered, a package in his hands.

"Mistress, this came with the evening post." He handed her the package.

"Thank you, Mr. Boyd. How are the footmen?" she inquired.

The butler straightened his shoulders with a natural air that demanded respect. "They will do. A bit rambunctious, but well-tempered lads."

She bit her lip to hide her smile. "Good. I'm glad to hear that." She studied the package in her hands, seeing the name of a hotel as the sender. "Mr. Boyd, who sent this?" she asked.

The butler hesitated. "Perhaps Mr. Hadley. He has been known to take rooms there when in London."

Owen? She sat up, despite the protestations of her body. Ever since she'd read the telegram, questions had been building, plaguing upon her mind and heart as she wondered where and what Owen might be doing. She would never have asked a servant anything in the past, not something so intimate about her husband, but she felt that she and Mr. Boyd were almost comrades in arms in the battle to restore Wesden Heath to its former glory.

She squared her shoulders and spoke. "Mr. Boyd, may I ask you something? I'm afraid it might be a bit personal, but it has to do with my husband. What do you know about Jack? Mr. Hadley received a telegram asking him to go to London to help someone named Jack. I assume it's Jack Watson? Owen mentioned him to me once, but I don't know very much about him."

Mr. Boyd cleared his throat, looking out a distant window on the opposite end of the library before replying. "Mr. Jack Watson has been a friend of Mr. Hadley's since they were boys. Fought in the war together. Mr. Watson even lived here for a time after the war but—"

"But what?" she pressed, digging her fingers into the arm of the chair. She felt she was close to something, to a realization of some bigger puzzle that was almost within reach.

"Please, Mr. Boyd. I need to know." It was the first time in her life she had begged for anything.

"Er...My apologies, Mrs. Hadley, but it's a sensitive matter and not fit for the ears of well-bred ladies."

Milly almost smiled at his protectiveness of her even in such a small way, but she needed the truth. "Mr. Boyd, I assure you, I am no fainting violet—please, continue."

He hesitated but after another pleading look from her he continued. "The summer that Mr. Watson spent at the Heath, Mr. Hadley had been engaged to a young woman in the village. There was some unpleasantness during that summer, and Mr. Watson left in the fall, just before Mr.

Hadley broke off the engagement and returned to London for a time."

"A young lady in town?" she echoed faintly, her ears ringing. "Would that young lady be Scarlett Brandon?"

The immediate flush in the butler's cheeks was the only answer she needed.

She had to wonder whether Owen had been telling her the truth. Had Scarlett truly fallen in love with another man? If she had, then why hadn't she married him? And had that man been Mr. Watson?

"Why did Mr. Watson leave Wesden Heath?" If Jack was the man Scarlett had been in love with, she needed to know why he'd left without marrying her. She knew a man didn't need a reason to abandon a woman; they did it all the time. But her instincts whispered there was a reason.

"I believe there was some discussion as to whether Mr. Watson believed himself a suitable match. You see, he suffers quite badly from soldier's heart, due to the war, mistress. He didn't wish to have a wife endure his melancholy moods."

"Oh...," she said, her heart twinging with a ghost of pain.

She couldn't forget the night Owen had woken up, a cold sweat dewing on his skin, muttering about needing forgiveness. He'd been choking on air and it had frightened her and saddened her. Was what Jack Watson faced somehow worse than that? If so, she might see how a man would hesitate to marry...

"Will that be all, mistress?" Mr. Boyd asked politely.

"Yes, thank you," she said. When she was alone, she studied the package, then carefully unwrapped it. It was a first edition of H. Rider Haggard's *Allan Quatermain*. A letter was tucked inside the front cover and she opened the book, instantly enveloped with the aroma of musty pages. A smell she adored, because it made her think of the library at Pepperwirth Vale. The letter was from Owen, and as she began to read, she could hear his voice, perhaps because she longed to hear him speak.

Milly,

I hope you're reading this. I hated the way we parted. I did not offer you a complete explanation of Mr. Brandon's comments, nor did I explain the reason for my hasty departure. I chide myself for both actions. As soon as I am able, I shall explain all of it to you. I thought to keep such things a secret, perhaps because in truth they are not my secrets to tell. But I know that truth must exist for us and I cannot keep the truth from you. There is much that lies between us, more than simply our marriage. I do not wish to damage what we are building. Please consider Allan Quatermain *a gift, a begging for your forgiveness. I realize you were forced to leave your own library behind. If you let me, I shall spend the rest of our lives filling Wesden Heath's library with every book your heart desires. I am not the most eloquent man when it comes to speaking from my heart, but I know that the thought of losing you fills me with a heavy ache. I shall write to you every day while away. Please, give me a chance to win your trust and to win your heart.*

Faithfully yours,

Owen

"Give me a chance to win your heart." She murmured the words aloud and realized her lips were trembling with a small smile. The man said he was not eloquent in matters of the heart, yet he was wooing her with his words.

She turned her attention again to his gift, stroking the spine of the book before she let herself peek at the first page. A good book had a way of erasing one's troubles, dulling one's ache, and lightening one's heart. She wanted to read it straightaway but knew she had something more important to do first.

A few minutes later, she had paper and pen, ready to write Owen back.

Owen,

If you have not realized by now, I am quite stubborn, but not lacking in sensibility. A few days before, I did not fully understand the situation. I am better informed now regarding Mr. Brandon and his sister as well as the truth you spoke to me regarding your involvement in the matter of her situation. Your duty is to care for Mr. Watson. Yes, I know everything. I was able to glean this information from

Mr. Boyd. Do not be cross with him. He betrayed no confidence. I shall remain here, with Allan, waiting for you to return. Please write to me every day as you promised. I shall write back.

Milly paused, then decided to add a quick note about the progress she'd made in the house and closed her letter with *Your Milly*. It felt silly, girlish even, but she couldn't bear to cross it out. She summoned one of the new footmen and gave him instructions to send it to London at Owen's hotel and then settled down to supper and reading.

It didn't erase her longing for him, or the fact that she'd grown fond of the way he'd tease her or challenge her to do or try things she normally wouldn't. There was more to it, though. He loved Wesden like she did Pepperwirth Vale. And seeing him so in love with a place made her feel like a kindred spirit with him. She nibbled a bite of her bread and tucked the blanket more firmly around her as she opened the novel again. The night seemed a little less lonely as she felt Owen's gift transport her to the distant lands of Africa.

Chapter Twelve

Ten days had passed since Owen had left Milly alone and gone to rescue Jack. He'd spent his time reading the responses that she'd sent him while Jack slept. Owen could scarcely believe that she'd actually written him back.

He leaned back against the bed in the hotel room while Jack packed his bag. Owen lifted the latest letter that had been received the night before. She had written him every single day, not even waiting for responses to his letters and he had done the same. He didn't want to think about the fortune he'd spent in hiring messengers to drive to Wesden and back with his letters.

The last letter unfolded in his hands and he read the words again, unable to keep from smiling.

Owen,

I finally cleared away a great mess in the attics. I would love to tease you about having bats in the belfry but I imagine you'd find some way to say I brought the bats with me from Pepperwirth Vale. It gave the maids quite a fright. They will need some persuading to clean up there. I do miss your teasing. I thought I would hate that most about you, that you would taunt me, but as always you prove me wrong. Do you know how frustrating that is for a woman who has sworn not to like the husband she was forced to marry? I suppose I'll have to forgive you for that.

Owen snorted. His Milly was forgiving him for ruining her. Now that he'd come to know her, come to really see who she was beneath her aloof façade...he would have chosen her over Rowena in a heartbeat if he'd had to do it all over again. He probably should never tell her that, though. He focused back on the letter.

How is Jack? I hope he's faring better. I believe bringing him home to Wesden might do him some good. We may both take care of him then. I miss you, and I'm afraid your parents' library is sorely lacking in literature. When you get home, you'll take me to town for books, won't you? Perhaps I might finally tempt you into reading She.

The ink had dried a little and then he'd seen a darker patch, as though she'd paused for a while and then started writing again.

I have been speaking to the schoolmaster of the little village Helena not too far from Wesden and I think he will let me assist in teaching the girls. It will take some convincing with their parents, but I should like to do this.

She was to achieve her dream, the one she'd whispered to him during one of the evenings after working themselves to death on the house and grounds. He hadn't dared laugh or scoff at her hopes of making the lives of other girls better. It had surprised him, but then he'd felt a burning pride in his chest at her hope to change the world, one child at a time. When he returned to Wesden, he would do everything he could to help her.

He brushed his thumb over the closing words of her letter.

Come home soon, husband. The nights are cold and lonely without you here.

Your Milly.

His face actually hurt from how much he was smiling. *My Milly.*

He carefully folded the last letter and collected the stack of remaining letters she'd sent, humming softly as he packed them into his coat pocket. Jack was placing shirts into a traveling case. He was still too pale, too thin, but his eyes were bright, and not with drink or fever.

"You truly want me to come home with you while you're settling in with your bride?" Jack flashed him a charming grin, a ghost of a smile that had broken many hearts, including Scarlett Brandon's.

"I do. What happened to you, Jack, that's within my power to stop. Therefore, you are coming back with me and what's more you will pay a visit to Ms. Brandon."

At this Jack froze. "Scarlett?"

Owen nodded as he collected his own travel case. "Yes. One visit. If you wish to see her again after that, I would be glad of that, but you owe the woman one visit."

During the last ten days, Jack had been wild, weak, screaming until his voice had broken, but with just one utterance of Scarlett's name and the man looked like a light breeze could have knocked him off his feet.

"I don't—" Jack raked a hand through his hair and shook his head.

"You will." Owen told him. "My wife and I argued over Scarlett because she didn't know the full story. You will visit Scarlett because you owe me."

Jack swallowed. "Very well. Are you ready?"

"Yes. The cab should be waiting for us."

He settled the hotel bill and then he and Jack climbed into the hired cab. The entire drive from London to Wesden, Owen rehearsed a thousand things in his mind and reread Milly's letters. In the last ten days, she had slowly opened herself up to him, shown that soft, compassionate, intelligent side, but he'd also seen what her father had said to look for. A partner. She had single-handedly reorganized the accounting of the house, hired new staff, and was restoring his childhood home to its former glory. How could he not appreciate a woman who was capable of doing that?

By the time the cab arrived at the house, it was late in the evening. Owen nudged Jack in the ribs, rousing his friend from sleep.

"What? Oh." Jack yawned and stretched before he climbed out ahead of Owen.

Mr. Boyd was there to meet them at the door. When they entered the hall, Owen halted. The lamps were dim but glowing, the musty scent was gone, the carpets looked bright, and the bannisters and floors were glossy with polish.

"Sir?" Boyd prompted, his dark brows lifting in concern and question.

"The house..." He knew Milly had been making progress, but he couldn't believe how visible the work was. Even the old grandfather clock by the base of the stairs was ticking away. The clock hadn't worked in years.

"Mrs. Hadley has been most effective, sir."

Owen laughed in delight. "I can see that." Having his home look warm and welcoming again...he hadn't thought it possible.

"Where is Mrs. Hadley?" He glanced around, disappointment knifing through him. He had hoped—foolishly so—that Milly would have been waiting up for him.

"The mistress is in the library, sir."

"The library?"

Mr. Boyd's face turned ruddy. "Yes, sir. She's taken to falling asleep in there every evening since you departed."

"Ahh…" Owen cleared his throat. "Why don't you see Mr. Watson settled and I shall go find her."

"Very good, sir." Mr. Boyd led Jack up the stairs while Owen removed his coat and gloves, handing them to a waiting footman. A new one he didn't recognize.

"What's your name?" he asked the lad.

"Stephen Parker, sir." The footman took the coat and gloves.

"Stephen, good to meet you. Would you have Cook send a dinner to Mr. Watson and a tray for two to my chamber?"

"Of course, sir." The lad dashed off.

Owen grinned at the younger man's exuberance before he headed to the library. It was the least used room in Wesden. His family had never been much into reading for leisure, but he had a new appreciation for it now. Having spent the last ten days helping Jack, watching over him as he got free of the influence of drink, Owen had been forced to read to pass the time. He'd sent Leo to the nearest bookshop to have him buy a collection of Haggard novels. He'd taken Milly's copy of *She* with him but wanted to read others by the same author. Reading *She* had changed him, or rather the way he understood Milly.

The story of *She* was beautiful, yet tragic. It was more than a simple entertaining novel. Milly had excellent taste in literature and he planned to let her build the library at Wesden into a room they would both enjoy.

When he reached the library, he found the door ajar. Firelight flickered against the walls and shelves as he nudged the door open. Milly slept curled up beneath a woolen blanket in a chair by the fire. Owen tread softly on the carpets as he approached her. Her hair was loose about her shoulders in luscious chestnut waves. His hands twitched with the need to bury his fingers in the soft coils. A book, the one he'd sent her, *Allan Quatermain*, was open on her lap. His lips curved into a smile as he leaned down, set the book aside, and collected his wife into his arms. He started walking and was halfway to his chamber when she stirred.

"Owen?" She covered her mouth as she yawned and blinked, gazing up at him. He adored her eyes, the way the bright blue could soften to such rich velvet black when she was in the dark.

"I didn't mean to wake you." He apologized just as they reached his bedchamber. Thankfully Evans was there, holding the door open to allow them in.

"Stephen just brought your food, sir. Nice and hot," Evans assured him before he nodded to the bed. "Constance laid out the mistress's nightdress for you. Ring if you need us."

"Good night, Evans." Owen lowered his wife to the bed and sat down beside her as Evans left and closed the door behind them.

"What time is it?" Milly sat up and attempted to comb her fingers through her hair.

"Late. I've only just got back. Jack is in a room down the hall."

At the mention of his friend, Milly reached out, placing one hand over his, the tender gesture making his heart swell.

"How is he? I couldn't tell much from your letters." Her searching gaze called to him, and he leaned over, brushing a kiss on her forehead.

"Better. He will stay here for a time, until I can be assured he won't fall back into bad habits."

She nodded and gave his hand a gentle squeeze.

"That was a very brave thing you've done. Mr. Watson is fortunate to have you as a friend."

He shrugged his shoulders. "Jack suffers more than I do. The war didn't simply scar him; it destroyed him. I feel as though..." His throat tightened and he turned his face away, unable to admit his secret shame. She would despise him for it.

"What? Please talk to me." She scooted closer and wrapped her arms around him from behind, resting her cheek on his shoulder. The embrace, so gentle and comforting, obliterated that last barrier inside him keeping his heart safe from her.

"When I see Jack, see how broken he is over what we faced during the war... and I come away with a few harmless nightmares, I can't help but wonder what that says about me. Is my heart so hard that the things that haunt him fail to haunt me? What sort of man am I, that my spirit is bruised rather than broken? We faced the same men, fought the same battles, our hands coated with the same innocent blood. Why am I not trapped inside the nearest bottle, too?"

Milly didn't speak for so long that he thought she wouldn't, but when she finally did, her voice was a delicate whisper close to his ear.

"When I first met you, I believed you were a heartless seducer, bent on securing a fortune."

He closed his eyes. Her vision of him was black and all too truc.

"But I was wrong. So very wrong." Her voice caught and she paused. "Everything you do comcs from a place of love. Love for your home, your friends, even your servants. I never met a man who acts with his heart as you do. The last thing you are is heartless."

He turned his head to look at her, and a little tear escaped one of her eyes and rolled down her cheek. He brushed a finger over the tear and leaned in to nuzzle her cheek.

"I want to kiss you right now. Would you let me?" he asked.

She nodded, bringing her arms around his neck as he shifted on the bed to face her.

"I'd like you to do a bit more than that, husband." A little impish smile curved her lips and warmed her eyes.

"Thank God." He chuckled against her lips right before he kissed her.

Her lips parted and he took advantage, thrusting his tongue into her mouth. She moaned in encouragement and met him kiss for kiss. Her hands dug at his clothes, tugging on his jacket, his shirt, the front of his trousers. Her clothes were a little trickier, and he had to slide one hand beneath her to unhook her skirt before she could shimmy out of it. He was never more desperate to get a woman fully bare beneath him than he was in that moment. Milly laughed, seemingly content to let him struggle with her clothing.

"Lend a hand, sweetheart?" he growled as he wrestled with the ties of her corset.

"Very well," she said, still laughing but breathless now. The expression lit up her face and her usually austere beauty was now soft and womanly. Her eyes were slumberous and her cheeks flushed to a delicate rose as she embraced their passion. He slowed to a stop, his hands knotted in her shoes as he stared at her in awe.

"What?" she asked, her brows drawing together, and her smile started to wilt at the corners.

"It's just..." He struggled for words. "You are so lovely it took my breath away." He meant it. Looking at her actually made him feel a tad light-headed.

Her lips formed an enchanting moue as she stared at him.

"Then why did you stop undressing me?" she asked, still confused.

He began undoing her laces again, this time more sure of himself. When he raised his gaze to hers, he was unable to stop a smug grin.

"I was savoring the fact that you are mine, my wife, mine to take to bed, mine to make love to." He parted the corset and she raised her arms as he lifted it off her. She was finally down to nothing but a filmy sleeveless chemise. Her full breasts were barely concealed beneath the thin material.

"It's time we got better acquainted with each other," he murmured with a wry chuckle before he lifted the chemise up and off her. Milly gasped, arms coming up to cover her breasts, but he caught her wrists and gently trapped them above her head while he nibbled a path to her breasts. He suckled each sensitive nipple until the small buds pebbled against his tongue. She panted beneath him, her sighs and moans of encouragement showing him what she enjoyed the most. He wanted to teach all of the delights to be had between a man and a woman.

Owen worked his way down her body, nipping and licking the curves of her breasts, the slightly rounded belly, and down to her mound.

"Owen, you can't!" Milly protested, but as he settled between her thighs, he saw excitement and fear flash through her eyes.

"Don't fear me. There will only be pleasure between us." He parted her womanly folds and licked her. Milly's hips jerked wildly as she nearly came up off the bed. The strangled little cry of pleasure made him chuckle. She was learning to respond to him without thought, to let her barriers down.

"Close your eyes," he murmured, and then continued to lick her, flicking his tongue inside her and swirling it in patterns. He braced himself on one arm and gently inserted one finger into her sheath, while he teased the little pearl peeping out from her folds. That was all it took to send her flying off the edge in a cry. She put her fist in her mouth to muffle the sound. Someday he'd teach her that she didn't have to silence her sounds of pleasure. Someday.

He crawled back up her body, feeling like a veritable god of ecstasy. She lay panting and gasping for breath beneath him, her lashes fluttering wildly.

"Want to try something different?" he asked.

"Different?" Her lips quivered as she still continued to breathe hard.

"Mmm." He dropped his head to kiss her neck and then bit down on her shoulder.

"Oh, that feels...nice," she moaned, her nails digging into his back as she dragged him closer. He positioned himself above her and sank inside. They shared a soft sigh of fulfillment as their bodies fully connected. But he didn't wait for her to move; he rolled their joined bodies so she lay atop him. She gripped his shoulders, staring down at him in shock.

"Me on top?" she asked, genuine surprise on her face. "Is this...acceptable?"

Owen lifted her hips, withdrawing, then jerked her back down, impaling her on his cock. She made a little whimper and smiled in a heated daze.

"It's acceptable, if you like how it feels. Do you?" he asked, and repeated the lift and thrust hard.

Milly bit her lip and nodded, starting to raise her hips on her own and slamming them back down. He kept a firm hold on her buttocks, giving one cheek a light tap with his palm. The tantalizing view of her breasts bouncing against his chest as they made love made it nearly impossible for him to focus on not coming too soon. This woman had the power to undo him and she had no idea how dangerous that was.

I've fallen for my wife. The thought struck him just as

he increased his upward thrusts and she dropped her hips down. They moved in time, their bodies working together in perfect sync. It was everything he'd ever dreamed to feel with a woman and it wasn't just about being in bed with her. What he felt right now came from something deeper, from the moments they'd shared leading up to this. The quiet smiles, the whispered words, the shared stories, their working together to resurrect his home to its former glory...Milly was perfect...for him. *How can I not love her?*

How could anything feel this good? Milly completely surrendered to the moment and her own passion.

"Give me your hands," she said.

Owen lifted his palms off her body and held his hands up by his face. She shifted a little, circling her hips, and grasped his hands, palm to palm. He laced his fingers through hers as she pinned their joined hands into the bed. They rocked together, eyes locked, sharing breaths. They began a delicious climb to pleasure. When she leaned down to kiss him, her body felt as though it burst apart in a thousand pieces before it came back together. She continued to kiss him long after he'd come beneath her.

There was little in the world she believed she'd ever

want to do forever, but kissing Owen, like this, while they were intimately joined, was one of them. Pure and simple. Nothing could ever be better than this. She finally understood why women risked scandal. It was so they would someday be free to act as men did to enjoy life, not be trapped by it.

Owen deepened the kiss and Milly clenched her inner walls around him, making him groan deeply. It seemed neither of them wanted to stop, but Milly was exhausted from another long day of helping with the house.

"Are you tired, sweetheart?" He squeezed their joined hands and she nodded, still trying to kiss him. "Then you need to rest." He rolled them so they lay on their sides facing each other.

"So do you." Her sleepy reprimand seemed to amuse him. He withdrew from her, but laughed softly as she made a disgruntled sound of protest.

"Oh dear, I've created a beast." He nuzzled his nose against hers.

"A beast?" She wrinkled her nose and frowned.

"An insatiable lovemaking beast." He kissed the tip of her nose.

Milly cuddled close, tucking her arms up by her chest as she burrowed into him.

"Owen, you promise not to leave again?"

"Leave?" He wound one arm around her waist.

She stroked his throat, needing to touch him. The

last ten days had seemed so empty, so lonely without him. She'd never needed a man to feel complete before, still didn't, but she'd grown to care about Owen...deeply, so much so that she'd feared she would be fully in love with him before long. What would he say in the morning? What would he do to make her laugh? What mischief would they get into while cleaning his home together? She longed for more time with him and having him back made Wesden Heath feel like home for the first time.

"No more running off to save people. I'd like to be a little selfish and claim you for myself. We never had a honeymoon, if you recall." She smoothed her hand flat on his chest above his heart, feeling a warmth so deep it stunned her as she counted his heartbeat.

"No more running off," he promised. When she looked up, his eyes were dark and fathomless.

"Owen, may I ask you something? I want an honest answer." His heart began to pound, and she licked her lips nervously.

"Honestly, that I can do. I've never been one to lie, except when necessary to prevent harm." He frowned, then continued. "Whatever you ask, I will always answer honestly." His arm around her waist squeezed slightly.

"When you realized it was me and not Rowena in the bed, were you very disappointed?" Asking him this felt like a knife was sliding between her ribs to cut her heart to ribbons, but it had been a lingering thought in her mind for a long time.

His heavy sigh filled her with so much dread she couldn't breathe for several long seconds, but she knew deep down from the start he'd wanted Rowena, not her. What she truly feared more than anything was that he still wanted Rowena but was doing the honorable thing by her and wouldn't stray, not even if his heart asked him to.

"I had set my sights on her; that much is true. If my valet hadn't made an error about which room she was in, I'd be with her now." He paused, his expression so serious that she knew what was coming next.

And here I was foolish enough to ask him to break my heart by telling me the truth.

"You would be happier then? If you ended up with Rowena?"

She didn't want to look at him, but she couldn't find the strength to turn away. His eyes softened and a hint of a smile played about his mouth.

"I'm sure we would have gotten along, but she isn't you. I don't want to be married to anyone else now that I've been with you."

His response was so unexpected that she blinked owlishly and gaped, openmouthed. He lifted his hand from her waist and used his fingers to close her mouth by gently tapping her under her chin.

"You don't believe me?" He laughed, sheer delight

making his eyes sparkle. At first she used to hate his teasing, but she'd realized now that it was part of how he showed affection, something she'd come to crave in the days they'd spent together. But his admission now, that he really wanted to be with her, filled her with a stirring of hope so strong that she couldn't speak.

She only managed to shake her head.

"Milly, sweetheart, you've seen how stubborn I am, how much help my home needed...I believe there is but one woman on earth who could handle me and my home. That woman is you. Rowena is a dear girl, but I need someone who can brave the wild with me, take me in hand when I act unreasonable, manage my household, see to my...passions." He added this last part with a little wink.

"You truly...like me?" She had never felt so vulnerable in her life. She'd managed to go her entire life without needing validation from anyone, especially a man, but Owen mattered. She ached to be cared for, liked back, as much as she liked him.

"I do." He kissed her, in a slow, lingering tasting, and she purred, sidling ever closer. She could have died from happiness. He liked her. It wasn't love. They hadn't been together long enough to love, but maybe someday...He was proving he was a partner in their marriage and that affection was growing between them. She'd never imagined she could have been so lucky to end up married to a man like him.

"What about me?" he asked.

"Hmm?" She didn't want him to stop kissing her.

Owen brushed a lock of hair back from her face. "Do you like me? I imagine you hated the idea of marrying me."

She couldn't help but laugh. "I thought my life had ended. You were so arrogant, so...full of trouble, but I am happy I was wrong."

"Full of trouble?" He bit her bottom lip, then kissed her again, flicking his tongue in and out until she was wet and squirming. This discussion was exciting her body all over again. Was it mad to be wildly in love with and hungry for one's husband? It certainly wasn't proper, but with Owen she knew she'd have to leave all propriety behind to enjoy life with him.

"Full of trouble sounds like it might be a good thing." He rolled her onto her back and slid between her parted thighs, thrusting inside hard and fast. The sensation of the sudden fullness made her gasp and arch her back. He didn't let up, the wild rush of this joining so different from what they'd done a short while ago. Clawing his back, she hissed in pleasure and nipped his neck. He growled and trembled above her, and she laughed against his skin. She never could have imagined this, a mating of two bodies so pleasurable that it bordered on the point of pain. She wanted more, so much more.

"Yes, Owen, yes," she whispered, her breathing ragged.

It wasn't just the sex she was agreeing to, but something more, something she was so afraid to say except to tell him yes. His answering reply dared to give her hope.

"Anything for you," he promised. In that moment, she believed him. She could have anything with him, and he with her.

Chapter Thirteen

The morning after Owen had come home, Milly awoke, smiling, and then wincing as her lower body protested with soreness. Last night had been wonderful, explosive, and certain more feminine parts of her were feeling the effects of her and Owen's bedplay. Despite the discomfort, she still grinned and let out a breathless giggle of pure happiness. She didn't regret anything. Last evening had been wonderful. Owen was home and they would be working side by side again. It truly felt like her home now, too.

The last week or so she'd worked alongside the staff to make Wesden Heath hospitable again, and the pride from knowing she'd helped to make a difference made her almost bursting with joy.

The bedroom door opened and Owen came in, holding a breakfast tray.

"Morning, sweetheart. I took the liberty of taking this from Constance so she could see to her other duties." He set the tray across her lap and kissed her lips.

"Thank you." Milly put one hand up to cover the spreading blush on her cheeks.

"I thought you might like to join me and Jack for luncheon before we go into town."

"You and Jack were planning to go to town?" It wasn't that she was jealous of Jack, but...he'd sworn last night to stay with her, to spend time with her after the last ten days apart. The last thing she wanted was to feel alone when her husband only lay beside her at night and spent no time with her during the day. Did that mean his only interest lay in her between the sheets? As pleasing as that was...she couldn't survive in a marriage based only on sex. She'd always wanted love and equality, not just physical intimacy, and she'd hoped that Owen was the same.

"I planned to only take you into town, but I realized we ought to force Jack to go with us. Fresh air being good for his constitution and all that. I was merely uncertain whether luncheon would interest you or not."

His reply made her heart flutter, but she tried to stay calm, not wanting him to know just how much that meant to her. She picked up a piece of toast and spread liberal amounts of marmalade over it. "What do you need to do in town?"

"Books. I'm afraid I read through most of the stack Hampton bought me while I was with Jack in London. My library here is quite lacking in decent novels. It's all political essays and historical treatises on various governments of France, Italy, and Spain. Not in the least bit interesting to me."

A giggle escaped her. "You're quite serious?"

He laughed and walked over to his dresser, where he opened the top drawer and pulled out a book. Her book. The copy of *She* that she'd been reading on their ride to Wesden Heath that first night.

"I finished this and need to return it to you." He held the book out to her, but when she reached for it, he leaned down to whisper against her lips a quote she had underlined with a pen.

"Yea, all things live forever, though at times they sleep and are forgotten."

Milly laughed and kissed him back before quoting from *Allan Quatermain*. *"Passion is like the lightning, it is beautiful and it links the earth to heaven, but alas it also blinds."*

The corners of his eyes crinkled with faint lines as he grinned.

"Hmmm...shall we spark a bit of lightning, wife?" He nibbled her lips as he rested one hand against the bed frame behind her. She curled her fingers into his shirt, holding him prisoner for more of those deep, all-consuming kisses of his. After several long moments, she let him go and their mouths parted with reluctance.

"Maybe later this evening we could continue this?" she asked hopefully.

He ran a thumb over her well-kissed lips. "There is no maybe; we *shall* continue this," he assured her.

"Good. Let me break my fast, then I'll join you and Jack in an hour."

Owen nodded. "Excellent. I'll be waiting." He kissed her forehead and left her alone to eat. She was famished and had no problem tucking away her meal before she rang for Constance.

After a bath and her usual morning ablutions, her maid helped her dress in a warm walking suit that had a long coat with military braiding.

"You look very smart, milady," Constance said, her eyes sharp with approval.

Milly smiled. She'd given up trying to remind Constance she was merely a gentleman's wife and no longer the daughter of a peer. She touched up her hair before Constance settled a large hat on her head with a navy-blue bow that matched the dark blue fabric of her walking suit. The skirt's train was a little fuller than the current style of hobble skirts, but she despised when fashion made a woman's mobility nearly impossible. Her skirt also enhanced her figure, taking the curves she possessed and displaying them leaner in places and fuller in others.

"Are the men ready for luncheon?" she asked, temporarily removing the hat now that she'd been assured it looked well with her suit.

"Yes, milady. They are waiting in the dining room."

"Thank you." She rose from her vanity and lifted her skirts with one hand while she headed for the door.

It would be her first time meeting Mr. Watson and she wished to make a good impression. He was one of Owen's closest friends, after all. She wanted to care about the people he cared about and for them to like her in return. In the past, she wouldn't have cared about making a good impression on a fortune hunter's best friend, but now that she really knew Owen and had seen into his heart, it mattered. Her nerves were a little frayed and she tried to quell the restless fleet of butterflies in her stomach. Would Jack like her? Would she like him? Surely they would get along; they both cared about Owen after all.

When she descended the stairs and walked toward the drawing room, she paused just outside the door at the sound of male voices. Her husband was laughing. The sound, heavens, the sound made her weak-kneed with desire and yet excited enough that if she spread her arms they might turn to wings so she could fly.

"She's convinced you to take up reading? Good God,

Owen, I ought to shake her hand or kiss the lady. I'm so glad someone finally forced you to enjoy the finer things in life. I used to love reading before..." He trailed off a little. The man's voice was low and rich, a bit like Owen's yet different.

That had to be Jack Watson speaking. The man liked to read. What else did she need to know that spoke well of his character? Nothing. A man who read was a man she could converse with.

"Milly has a way of making me see things differently," Owen said.

"I can see that." This time Jack laughed, the sound no less pleasant, even though it didn't affect her the way Owen's had.

She chose that moment to enter the room, lest she be discovered eavesdropping on them.

"Ahh, there you." Owen came over to greet her, grasping her gloved hands in his as he kissed her on the lips, right in front of their guest. Her face flamed, but she couldn't help it; she always responded to him strongly.

"Mrs. Hadley, I'm delighted to make your acquaintance." Jack came around the table to greet him. It was the first chance Milly had to get a good look at him. He was tall like Owen, but thin. She could see he'd once been a muscular man, full of strength. He might yet regain that strength, but it would take time, food, and physical activity. Yet despite his slightly diminished state, he still had a reserved sort of charm some men possessed, a quiet dignity that drew friends and influenced people. Owen was more like a bright fire to Jack's single flame. Both burned hot, but in different ways.

"Mr. Watson, I'm so glad you're here." Milly smiled and leaned a little into Owen as she spoke, hoping he'd see her touch as supportive. "My husband needs a friend to keep him busy and entertained lest he get in the way of my restorations to the house."

Jack snorted. "I highly doubt he has any need of being entertained while you are around. He talked of nothing but you while he..." Jack coughed, his face paling as he seemed to realize he'd confessed too much. "Well, I'm sure he's told you how he's helped me."

She nodded, her smile fading. "Yes. And we are both glad you're feeling better." She meant it.

"I am." He patted his stomach. "Wesden Heath has one of the best cooks in this part of the Cotswolds. I'll likely outgrow my trousers if she keeps preparing such meals as I had last night."

Milly had to agree. Cook kept things simple, but hearty and tasty. She'd come from a world of ten-course meals with elaborate dishes and exotic garnishes. Expensive tables were displayed as a sign of Pepperwirth wealth. Wesden could not have been more different. Her old self would have been rankled at the idea of modest dishes and a home in great need of repairs, but marrying Owen had changed her. Being around him had made her see things different, value different things.

"Shall we sit?" Owen offered, and they took their seats at the dining room table.

Luncheon was brought in by a footman, a young man named Jennings who was another of the new staff. He grinned, as though delighted in his job, but when he saw Milly watching him he quickly wiped the expression from his face. That was something else that had changed inside her. She would have been disapproving of a servant who had caught her attention in such a manner, but after spending the last two weeks of working with them, she'd gained a sense of camaraderie. When Jennings looked her way again, she offered him a small smile and he beamed at her.

After the young man left, she turned her attention back to Jack and Owen. She froze when she saw her husband watching her, his eyes hot with desire, and there was a softer, subtler emotion shadowing the desire that she couldn't quite read. She ducked her head and focused on her meal, trying to ignore how exposed she felt. In many ways, it was like the night when they had dinner at Hampton House, but without the anger and resentment that had been between them. This was...a heated exchange born of affection. Milly couldn't help but smile as she finished her lunch.

When she, Owen, and Jack were ready to leave, she

collected her hat from Constance, who helped pin it on her head before she met the men at the front door. A hired cab was waiting for them.

"You know," she leaned in to Owen to whisper, "we can afford one of our own now." The money she'd brought to the marriage could certainly cover a car and so much more.

He glanced down at her in surprise. "Only if you wish it. I wouldn't make such an expensive decision unless you wanted it, too. It's your money, Milly."

Milly stumbled but Owen caught her by the waist and kept her upright. She was stunned. Hadn't it always been his intention to marry solely to gain access to his wife's funds? What had changed?

"But I thought—"

With a shake of his head, he cut her off. "My desire, my hope, was that any woman I married would love my home enough to make the costly decisions herself. I never planned to spend your money without your permission or counsel."

And just like that, tears stung her eyes. She was going to cry right there in front of him and Jack, like some silly ninny. That had been one of her darkest fears, that she would be trapped into marriage solely for monetary gain by a husband who would not see her as an equal and use her money without consulting her. Yet here Owen was, defying every awful expectation she'd had, except one. He did not love her, or if he did, he hadn't yet told her. She wanted love, wanted it so much she'd forced herself to believe she could never have it, that life wouldn't give her that one true dream.

Could Owen's like someday turn to love? Her inner voice was that of a younger girl, the one who'd lived in France and dreamed of a man loving her as much as she did him, as equal partners in love and life.

"What's the matter, sweetheart?" He motioned for Jack to go on ahead of them to the car while he remained on the steps, holding her close. He cupped her face, wiping away a rebellious little tear that dared to drip down her cheek.

"It's nothing." She flashed him a falsely bright smile. "Would you kiss me?" she asked.

He chuckled. "It would be my greatest pleasure, wife." He bent his head and stole her breath with a heady kiss that made her float on air. How could he always do that? Seize her heart and body with just a kiss?

"Cab's running. You two better get down here so we can go to town." Jack's hooting laugh made them break apart, sharing shy smiles.

"Tonight." Owen promised everything in that one word.

"Tonight," she agreed.

Chapter Fourteen

Owen followed behind Milly as she nearly skipped ahead of him down the narrow gravel lane. The rows of houses leading into the village of Wesden looked like cozy little stone structures, each with painted doorways and puffs of smoke from their little chimneys. In the spring and summer a dozen bright colors would coat the windowsill flower boxes, and ivy would climb the walls of the home. The idyllic setting would capture Milly's heart as it had his so long ago as a boy.

Every few steps Milly would turn to face him, beaming. Her smiles were so much freer now, as though the façade she'd clung to for years was at last crumbling. When they'd left the house after luncheon, she'd looked so lost, so frightened, and he couldn't figure out why. Kissing her had been an easy thing, something he'd come to adore, but he wondered why she seemed to need reassurance that he belonged to her fully and completely. She didn't need that. He'd vowed he was hers, would always remain faithful.

"Owen." Milly paused by a flower shop as they reached the village proper. "Might we buy some flowers? I should like to start a hothouse garden. We could construct something in the spring. If we buy a few plants, I could tend to them indoors through the winter."

He took long strides to catch up to her.

"What a charming idea, wife." He tucked her arm in his as they entered the small shop.

A brass bell jingled merrily above their heads, and Milly immediately began an intense examination of the flowers. Owen was content to watch her, drinking each expression that crossed her face as she removed her long gloves, touched bare skin to petals, and bent to inhale a particular flower. He came up behind her when she paused in front of a row of orchids. He touched a purple orchid inches from her hand.

"Do you know why these flowers are considered scandalous?" he whispered into her ear. His other hand touched her hip, gripping her in a gentle but possessive hold.

Milly's breath caught and she held still. "No, why?" she whispered.

"Because"—he paused, relishing the way he knew she would react when he spoke his next words—"they resemble a lady's folds...the silken texture, the rich color, the opening ready for penetration." He stroked the orchid's petals in an intentionally seductive manner and chuckled when Milly's breath quickened.

"You're wicked, you know that? Positively wicked," she hissed, but when he nuzzled her cheek, he felt her lips curve up in a smile.

"When we get home, I'll stroke your orchid," he promised huskily.

She jabbed him lightly in the ribs, making him step back and clear his throat.

The florist was watching them with wide eyes, and Milly blushed and tried to fix her gloves, attempting to pretend nothing had happened between them.

As distracted as he was by thoughts of seducing his wife, he couldn't help but wonder how Jack was doing. The excursion into town had nothing to do with the shopping. Jack had finally agreed to meet with Scarlett Brandon at one of the pubs. It was a tad improper, but Owen was not sure she would have agreed to come back to Wesden to meet Jack. It would have seemed awkward for his former fiancée to meet with his best friend under his roof.

"You're worried about Mr. Watson, aren't you." Milly's gentle but accurate observation dragged him out of his thoughts.

"Yes," he admitted. "The man has been through hell and I'm not sure he can handle Scarlett or her situation."

"You mean the baby she lost?" Milly curled her arm in his and pointed at several flowers. The shopkeeper hastened to prepare a few cuttings for her to take with them.

Owen blew out a breath. "I can't begin to imagine what losing a life inside you does to a woman. It must be hellish, and for a man like Jack, he's so sensitive, so good and kind, it might break him when Scarlet tells him about the miscarriage. But he needs peace in that part of his life."

Milly leaned into him, trying to comfort him. She probably had no idea that she was doing something like that; it was a tender gesture, one she would probably not have done had they not been as intimate as they'd become in the last two weeks. He felt so close to her and he had the strangest urge to ask her a question that surprised even himself.

"Are you interested in having many children?" he asked softly. He'd never asked or wanted to ask a woman about that, and he was oddly nervous and excited at the prospect.

Milly lifted her gaze to his, and he reveled in the startled, wide-eyed look there in her blue depths.

"Children?" The one word escaped breathlessly from her lips.

"Yes," he chuckled. "How many do you want?"

"Well, I...," she sputtered, then blushed. "I don't know. At least two?" She sounded so adorably unsure, and it made him suddenly desperate to get her into bed, or possibly on the nearest flat surface. He liked it when she was flustered, especially when he was the cause.

"Milly...," he purred, leading her to the door of the shop. "Why don't you and I go to the nearest inn and rent a room—"

"What about the flowers?" she interrupted, her voice still breathless.

"Mr. Tabor, put them on my account, and I'll send a lad here tomorrow to fetch them."

"Very good, sir." Mr. Taber was smiling a knowing smile as he turned away.

"Come on, we can find a way to occupy ourselves while we wait for Jack." He nuzzled her cheek and stole a lingering kiss. Every time he touched her, his blood heated and a soft warmth filled his chest. It had never been like that with any other woman.

"I might be tempted." Milly's blue eyes sparkled with her own rising passion.

"Then let's go find us a bed."

"Owen!" she gasped, but her delighted smile was all the encouragement he needed. They were halfway to the inn when Owen spotted Jack striding toward them. His face was ashen and his eyes were wide and stark with pain.

"Jack?" he asked, pausing Milly by curling an arm around her waist.

"I need to return to Wesden Heath immediately," Jack said, shoving his hands into his coat pockets.

Owen exchanged glances with Milly. "You're ready to return home?"

Milly nodded, her lips pursed in a thin line.

"Jack, I really think—"

"Now, Hadley." A silent rage tainted with pain colored his eyes.

Owen signaled their cabdriver who'd waited for them at the edge of town. The cab ride home was tense. Jack stared morosely out the window and Owen exchanged glances with Milly, but neither of them said anything.

A prickling sense of unease rippled through Owen as he and Milly followed Jack upstairs when they were back at the house. Something wasn't right. He caught his wife by the arm and held her back.

"Wait a moment. Let me have a private word with him."

She nodded. "Let me know if you need me." She squeezed his hand before she let go and a sudden impulse to seize her and kiss her again swept over him. He pulled her into his arms, kissing her hard and deep. It was as though someone had trod over his grave and he was filled with a terrible sensation that he might never see her again. It was foolish; she was here. They were married. There would be nothing to take him away from her. Even reminding himself of that did not make it any easier to let go. She'd become a lifeline for him in the last two weeks, keeping him afloat through a storm he hadn't realized he was caught in.

"Is everything all right?" Milly whispered in his ear.

"Yes, I'm sure it's fine." He gave her one last hug before he forced himself to let go.

He walked to Jack's room, not bothering to knock. They were going to have a talk whether Jack wanted to or not. When he turned the handle and swung the door open, he froze.

Jack was standing by the window of his room, his suitcase lying open, items scattered on the four-poster bed. As Owen sought out Jack, the thinner man turned to him.

"Don't come any closer, Owen," he said softly. The sunlight coming in through the window behind him glinted off something in his hand.

Owen's entire body seized with tension as he recognized a pistol in his friend's hand. "Jack...," he demanded, but didn't move. "Jack, what are you doing?"

His friend slowly turned to look at him, tears shining in his eyes. "Did you know, Owen? About the baby?" A hint of accusation followed his question.

Owen hesitated, wondering how to answer. He and Jack fought side by side, covered in blood and sweat beneath the distant African sun. You couldn't lie to a man, not after sharing that experience.

"I knew. She came to me after you left, begged me to cry off because she couldn't be married to anyone but you. Then she lost the baby."

Jack stroked his hand over the pistol, and the November sun, bright and bold, flashed like quicksilver off the metal.

"I should have been there for her, helped her with the baby. I'm a damned coward. A d-damned coward." The sound of his voice cracking beneath his pain tore out Owen's heart.

"No, you're not," he argued. Something inside him was fracturing, a wall of strength he'd built to keep the memories of the war at bay all these years.

"I was a medic, Owen. I couldn't save enough men, and I killed so many others...I'm not fit to draw breath." There was an awful finality to his tone that made Owen's blood run cold.

Jack raised the pistol toward his head.

Owen reacted. Years of living softly in London had not dulled his instincts. He lunged for Jack just as the barrel of the pistol reached his head. Their bodies collided and the gun dropped down to the ground next to them as they crashed to the floor.

"Let me die," Jack moaned as his fingers closed around

the gun. Owen clamped a hand around his wrist, their eyes meeting.

"You never left me behind. I'm not about to leave you."

Tears stung Jack's eyes as he continued to struggle, kicking Owen hard in the stomach. Air rushed out of his lungs as he grabbed at the gun between them—

Bang!

MILLY WAS HALFWAY DOWN THE STAIRS WHEN the loud bang of a gunshot froze her dead in her tracks, one foot raised, one hand still holding her skirts up.

A gunshot. The sound finally registered and she screamed. Jumping into motion, she spun and fled back up the stairs, racing for Jack's rooms. The door was ajar. The sight that met her eyes would haunt her for the rest of her life.

Owen lay on the floor, one hand over his stomach, bleeding, gasping softly, his eyes wide and dazed. Jack sat against one bedpost, holding the gun and staring in horror at his friend.

"Owen!" Milly ran to her husband and knelt by his side as he struggled for breath. When she jerked her head toward Jack, her eyes blurred with tears. Panic crashed in around her but she struggled to stay afloat. She had to be strong for Owen.

"Jack what happened?"

"I was trying to end my life…The fool tried to stop me. Damn you, Owen, damn you!" Jack shouted, tears streaming down her face.

Owen clutched Milly's hand, gasping and whispering her name.

"Milly…"

"Shh…" She tried to calm him down before she looked at Jack again. "Weren't you a medic during the war? Can't you do something? Anything?"

Suddenly Jack's panicked expression hardened and he nodded curtly, dropping the gun on the floor with a *thunk* as he suddenly straightened.

"Yes, yes, I can!" He rushed over to his suitcase and pulled out a small medical bag. While he sorted through items, laying them out on the bed, Milly turned her attention back to Owen.

"Milly." The one name was so soft she barely heard it. He could die. Her husband. How could he do that to her? Not after she was foolish enough to go and fall in love with him.

I love him…

"Owen." She cupped his face between her hands, and his eyes focused on her as she bent over him.

"Owen, I love you. Do you hear me? I love you and if

you…" Fear and anguish squeezed her throat closed for a moment and she couldn't breathe.

"Please, Owen, fight to stay with me." There was still pain in every syllable, but she felt her own strength, too. She would fight to keep him and he needed to fight to stay with her.

He swallowed hard, his breath short. "You were the best thing…in my life." He seemed to struggle hard to get the words out. Once he'd said them, his head dropped to the ground and his eyes closed.

"No!" she screamed. "Don't you dare leave me!" Tears pooled so thick in her eyes she couldn't see.

"Jack, he's…"

Jack knelt beside her, his gray eyes sharp and clear. "Put pressure on his stomach. Can you do that?" The cloud of depression and listlessness was gone from him.

"Yes." Milly did not like the sight of blood, but she could do this for Owen. She pressed the heels of her palms on the wound.

"Good." Jack lifted several tools up. "I'm going to lift him and see if the bullet lodged in his back or if it passed through." He lifted one edge of Owen's shoulder and pressed a hand beneath him, then frowned.

"What is it?" Milly demanded.

"Didn't pass through. I'll have to dig the bullet out."

"What?" Milly's stomach rolled violently.

"Go fetch some brandy or scotch. Any type of stiff alcohol will do."

Milly stood and rushed from the room. Mr. Boyd, Mrs. Nelson, and the entire house were gathered outside.

"Owen's been shot. We need someone to go to the village and fetch a doctor immediately. And we need alcohol and clean cloths."

"What about hot water?" Mrs. Nelson suggested as Mr. Boyd issued further orders.

"Yes!" Milly nodded before rushing back into the room.

Jack had stropped Owen's shirt off in the minute she'd been in the hallway and he was heating his scalpels in the fire.

"Sterilization," he hastily explained. Milly didn't care. She dropped down beside Owen, clasped one of his hands, and brought it to her lips, kissing his palm, his knuckle, anything to give him comfort, even though she knew he probably couldn't feel it.

Mrs. Nelson entered and handed Jack a bottle of gin. He dosed several cloths with it and handed them to Milly.

"Wash his wounds and then I'll dig out the bullet."

Milly wiped at the blood, clearing the red, inflamed wound. Once that was done, Jack cut into her husband's stomach with the scalpel, digging; the sound of blood and flesh shifting made Milly wince and fight back more tears. And then she saw it, the dull gleam of the lead ball as Jack worked it up to the surface. He deftly removed the ball and dropped it in a small metal tin Milly hadn't even noticed he'd put next to his supplies.

"Clean the wound again," Jack instructed. She did as he told her, and then she kept hold of Owen's hand as Jack used a metal needle and thick dark thread. He stitched the wound, but Milly couldn't watch that. She stroked bits of Owen's dark hair out of his face and held her breath.

"Will he make it, Mr. Watson?" Mrs. Nelson asked. She clutched the bottle of gin to her bosom, her eyes wide and anxiety creating tense lines around her mouth.

Jack placed two fingers on Owen's bare wrist and pulled out a silver pocket watch. For a full minute he studied the watch and held Owen's wrist.

"His pulse is steady. A little weak, but I think he stands a good chance. Stomach wounds are usually fatal but sometimes the bullet passes through a spot that misses all vital organs. From what I could tell, we're damned lucky it's the latter. It's blood loss and infection we need to watch for now." Jack glanced around, then called out, "Mr. Boyd, get a few strong lads to help me lift him onto the bed. We'll clean the wound once more and bandage him up." Jack wiped his hands off on a spare cloth and turned to Milly, gently prying her grip off Owen's hands.

"Let them get him all settled." Jack's voice was soothing, doctorly, and she nodded, letting go of Owen's hand.

She clenched her hands together as she watched the men lift Owen and put him on the bed. Mrs. Nelson volunteered to clean the wound and helped Jack bandage him up. Once she had gotten it all cleaned, Milly perched on the bed beside Owen and clasped his hand once they had tucked him beneath the covers. Jack remained with her, sitting in a chair opposite the bed, his eyes still sharp and clear. Silence lay thick between them and she almost thought he wouldn't say anything.

"I'm so sorry I've done this to you, Milly. To you and Owen."

She blinked and wiped at her eyes. "Owen told me some of what it was like during the war. I cannot begin to know how hard that must be to live with." She paused and raised her gaze to his. "But you owe it to yourself not to take the coward's way out. There are people here to help you. Owen, the Earl of Hampton, me. You have friends who love you enough to fight you for a gun. You owe it to them, too, to fight every day for happiness." *Like I have.* She realized as she spoke that in the few weeks since she and Owen had married, they had struggled and successfully won some measure of happiness together.

"It wasn't the war that made me lose myself." Jack dragged a hand through his hair and his eyes drifted to the window, as though seeing something she could not.

"You mean Scarlett and the baby." She didn't make it a question.

Jack shrugged one shoulder, but the quiet grief in his eyes tore at her heart as she finally nodded.

"Would you take my advice, Jack?" They'd been through so much in the last hour she knew they were beyond the formality of last names.

"I'm listening." He focused on her again.

"You still have a chance to live a life, possibly with Ms. Brandon. She begged Owen to release her from their engagement well after you'd gone. And it had nothing to do with the baby. She is still holding her heart for you. Trust my feminine instincts."

A glimmer of hope, a tiny one, flickered in his eyes.

"I'll keep that in mind." He stood and glanced at the door. "I'll go have a word with Mrs. Nelson and have her send some food up for you while I wait for the town doctor."

Milly nodded and watched him leave. The burden on her heart eased slightly. After a few minutes, Owen's hands suddenly tightened around hers, and his eyes opened.

"Milly?" He choked out her name in a soft gasp.

She leaned closer, trying to put her face in his line of sight.

"I'm here." She brushed an unruly lock of hair back from his eyes. "I'm here, Owen."

He smiled and nodded. "I'm not dead." He chuckled and then winced. "Must have passed out from blood loss and pain." He attempted to sit up, but Milly pressured a hand on his shoulder.

"Stay down, you stubborn man," she huffed. "You were shot."

"I'm not likely to forget that." He reached over and touched her hand, covering it with his. When their gazes locked, she was swept away by the tide of emotions.

"I meant what I said." His tone was soft, but each word was clear and firm, her heart skipping a painful beat.

"Meant what?" she finally dared to ask.

"That you were the best thing in my life. *You are*," he amended, smiling.

The bashful expression on a naturally seductive man stirred deep, confusing feelings in her. She was so used to his wicked smiles, ones intended to make her want to strip out of her clothes and climb into bed with him, but this smile...it was so much more...It was a smile of love, not seduction.

She hadn't forgotten what she'd told him as she thought he was dying. *I love you*. She couldn't deny it, but accepting it was terrifying. What if he didn't love her back?

She couldn't—

"Milly." Owen sighed wearily and was pushing himself up into a sitting position before she could stop him. He swayed, cursed softly, and favored his stomach before he met her gaze.

"What?" she replied, trying to hide that she was hurting inside as much as he seemed to be on the outside.

"I can see you thinking too hard." He grasped her hands and brought them to his lips, kissing them. "If you haven't realized how completely I've fallen for you, then you aren't as bright a woman as I thought you were." One corner of his sensual lips slid into a crooked grin that made her squirm inside in shock and delight. Fresh tears stung her eyes and burned the tip of her nose.

"You love me?" *Please, just let me hear him say yes.* She sent the prayer into the wide world on silent wings of hope.

His hazel eyes focused on her lips as he brushed a fingertip over them.

"How could I not love you? You're bright, beautiful, and compassionate. An equal partner in all things. A man like me could never be luckier to have a woman like you in my life, in my bed," he added with a roguish wink, before he turned serious again. "You're in my heart, so deep I cannot get you out. My love for you is a part of my soul now." He cupped her cheek and closed the distance between them, sealing his life-altering words with a kiss. One that stole her breath, her heart; every part of her fell that much deeper in love with Owen. He nibbled her lips gently, sweetly, before the kiss deepened. Their tongues playfully danced and his good arm curled around her waist. Only when Owen winced did their mouths part.

"I'm so sorry," she gasped, hurting to see him in pain.

He chuckled. "It will heal."

"Yes," she echoed. "It had better."

Owen shook his head, eyes glinting with barely suppressed mirth. "Oh, how I love your commanding spirit, dear wife."

She knew now he was teasing her. It was his way, always had been, of saying three little words. *I love you*.

Leaning into his good shoulder, she rested her head there, playing with their fingers, lacing them together.

"I command you to be happy, dear husband," she teased him back.

"As you wish. Only so long as you are with me. *Always*." His voice was still rough with emotion and she couldn't resist stealing one more kiss.

He surrendered his heart and she had done the same. For love, for each other, they would do anything.

Thank you for reading *A Gentleman Never Surrenders*. Turn the page to read the first two chapters of *A Scottish Lord for Christmas* which is about Milly's little sister Rowena and the dashing Scottish earl, Quinn.

A Scottish Lord for Christmas

CHAPTER 1

England, October 1911

Rowena Pepperwirth dashed along the lawn of the winter-browned grass of the Hampton House gardens. A gust of wind wrenched her hat from her head but she didn't stop running to chase it. Terror gripped her heart and blood pounded a violent tempo in her ears.

There was only one thing that mattered. A little girl in a blue dress and white pinafore, who could not be older than three, was climbing onto a stone fountain edge about fifty feet away. A fountain Rowena had seen up close only yesterday and which she knew with dreaded certainty had a very slick ledge...The icy water inside was thickly dotted with lily pads. If the child fell, she could drown as she scrambled to get free of the watery vegetation.

A distant roar filled her ears and her palms slickened with sweat as she raced down the garden path.

Please don't fall, please...She prayed she could reach the little girl in time. The distance between her and the fountain seemed infinite. The child could die if she wasn't fast enough...

Leaning forward, Rowena pushed her legs until they burned as she sprinted toward the child. She slid straight into the stone base, her knees smarting from the impact, but she ignored it while she grasped the girl by the back of her dress.

The surge of fear didn't fade immediately. Hands shaking, Rowena was immobile, holding the child above the water for a second before she recovered from the shock.

The little girl bounced and squealed, clapping her chubby little hands and peering into the fountain.

She was safe.

Rowena tugged her back into her arms, wrapping herself around the child protectively. Her hands shook and she had trouble breathing. It was all right. She'd gotten there in time. Shutting her eyes, she held the girl close, never more thankful she was fast on her feet.

"Fishes!" The little girl jabbed a delicate little finger at the water.

Rowena smiled and nuzzled the girl's cheek before kissing her. "Indeed, there are fish when it's warmer, but we mustn't catch them. You might fall in and then what would happen to you?" She feathered her fingers through the girl's curls, marveling at the way the light played upon strands as perfect as spun gold.

"No fishes?" the child queried solemnly, looking now at Rowena in a knowing way.

"No fishes."

"Thank 'eavens, miss!" A middle-aged nurse trundled round the corner of the nearest hedgerow, her face red and her breath uneven as she struggled to speak. "Wee bairn escaped me, she did." The woman's Scottish accent caught Rowena by surprise. Scots were common enough in London but in the countryside they were rare. She'd known that one of the guests at the Earl of Hampton's house party was Scottish, but she hadn't realized he'd brought a nurse with him or that he had a child. Then again, mentioning one's children in the midst of a house party wasn't done. Babes stayed in the distant nurseries, which saddened Rowena. She adored children. One of her dearest dreams was to have a brood of children running about her house someday.

"It's quite all right. I have her. She's safe." Rowena curled an arm around the child's waist, smiling as the little girl bounced excitedly and pointed at the few solitary fish that had so far survived the increasingly cold weather. Their sleek silver bodies ducked and dove in the murky depths of the fountain, and she watched them in fascination and single-minded determination.

"Papa!" the babe pronounced excitedly, and jabbed a little index finger toward the house.

"Is your papa here, little one? I'm sure he'd be worried to know you ran off without him. Fathers worry about their daughters. You must take care not to frighten him." The child's eyes, a soft dove gray, fixed on Rowena as though considering seriously what she'd said, and then she dropped onto her bottom on Rowena's lap, content to simply watch.

The nurse eased down onto the lip of the fountain base beside them, her face still flushed. "The wee one has fast legs, just like her father did when he was a bairn. Could never catch that child." The nurse's face was gentle with tenderness as she said this.

"Is she Lord Forres's child?" Rowena queried.

It had to be the man she'd met at dinner the previous night. The quiet, well-spoken, and all-too-handsome Earl of Forres had been the object of quite a few stolen glances from the ladies over the various courses at dinner. Rowena, only eighteen, was certain it wasn't proper for so many women to be sneaking looks at a man far down the table from them. But as this was her first official house party since her come-out in London a few weeks before, she wasn't quite sure if the social rules were different between London and the country. Naturally that meant she'd been glancing at him too. It was impossible not to. He was incredibly handsome, with intense eyes and a soft smile that did strange things to her body whenever he'd met her gaze. And the way he moved—in that graceful yet powerful way—had drawn every female eye to him over and over again.

"Aye, she's his all right." The nurse chucked the little girl under the chin and the child giggled.

Rowena held her breath as she stared down at the girl. She shared her father's serious gray eyes, but her light blond hair was a contrast to her father's dark brown locks. Did she take after her mother, then? Rowena didn't know much of Forres except that he was twenty-eight and well in-laid when it came to property and money.

That did not matter so much to her. Rowena's family was well off and titled, so she had no need to look for a wealthy husband. This left her free to enjoy meeting someone she would like to marry. She focused on the men themselves and not the social positions she could gain. She wanted to be viewed equally, as a partner, not a subordinate. Unlike her sister Milly, who dreaded the idea of marriage, Rowena looked forward to the challenges of sharing a life with someone and raising children, but she knew she had to choose the right person. Someone who would see her value and trust her to bring something to their marriage besides simply childbearing abilities.

That was why Forres had intrigued her the previous

evening. When he spoke, his rich, dark voice had an enticing Scottish lilt that seemed to curl in the air like a slow, dancing plume of smoke, mesmerizing her. The candlelight had illuminated his eyes and she hadn't been able to look away as he talked. His opinions on politics and social issues were well informed and he approved of women being equal to men. He was neither proud nor so opinionated as to alienate anyone during polite conversation. Even Milly, Rowena's older headstrong sister, had been impressed with Forres.

"I didn't know Lord Forres had a child. I thought he was unmarried."

There certainly hadn't been a wedding band on his finger. Little whispers had traveled down the table, escaping from behind the edges of water goblets as the ladies had passed along their observations to each other. The fact that he wasn't married had provoked quite the discussion among the women after the men had gone off to smoke cigars and drink. She'd taken to looking at him, and more than once his eyes had touched upon hers, making her feel dizzy. There was something about him, the curve of his lips in a hint of a smile, the intensity of his gray eyes as he watched her. It had made her body flush with heat.

"Aye, he's only got the one. Our countess passed a year ago and my lord's been sore for missing her." The older woman's face was somber as she spoke, and for a moment she was quiet. But then a little smile crept back onto her lips. "But now he's wife hunting." The nurse winked at her conspiratorially.

Wife hunting? She could just picture the darkly handsome earl prowling through the underbrush, rifle at the ready to hunt ladies who fluttered in autumn-colored gowns like a dozen pheasants. The image was silly enough to make her bite her lip to hide her smile. But then she focused on what the nurse had said. Forres *had* been married. His wife had died.

Rowena cuddled the excited child closer in her arms as she realized the little babe had no mother. All children should know a mother's love. She squeezed the girl in a hug. Rather than squawk as other children might, the little girl ceased her bouncing and settled more firmly in Rowena's lap. It felt...right in a way Rowena couldn't explain, and her longing for children of her own grew even stronger.

"She likes you. Blair doesn't like most women and hasn't had a chance to be around too many besides myself and the staff." The nurse was smiling widely now, a glimmer of hope in her eyes that Rowena didn't understand.

"Blair?" Rowena said, and the little girl lifted her head to stare back.

"That's me!" The child beamed at her.

"Nice to meet you, Blair." Rowena smiled back, then

turned her attention to the nurse. "He's wife hunting here in England? Why not take a bride closer to home?"

"I suppose," the nurse mused, "he doesn't want someone that reminds him of the previous Lady Forres. He doesn't share much of his heart; he's quiet, but a good man. He needs his heart healed. A good woman would do well for him."

Rowena brushed her fingertips over the curls by Blair's cheeks, tousling them. They were as soft as silk and as fine as a baby bird's feathers. She pondered over the nurse's speculations. Lord Forres was hunting for a wife to heal his broken heart? Her own heart twinged in pain at thinking of how lonely he must be. He sounded like a man who loved deeply. Rowena couldn't help but feel drawn to him now, knowing he bore such pain. It was rather romantic, in a sad way.

Before she could speak again, a man burst around the hedgerows, sprinting toward them. It was Lord Forres. His dark hair was in wild tangles about his head as though he'd dragged his hands through the strands, and his lips were peeled back in an almost feral snarl.

He skidded to a halt just a few feet away when he spotted the nurse first.

"Mrs. Finch!" he bellowed at the nurse. "Where the devil have you been? I've searched the entire house for you and Blair..." As he stared at his child, safe in Rowena's arms, the wild look in his eyes softened slightly.

"She's safe, my lord," Rowena said as she stood, tucking Blair against her right hip.

"Papa!" The little cherub smacked her hands together, wriggling in Rowen's hold.

"Oh, my wee heart." The earl strode over to Rowena and plucked Blair out of her arms before she could even protest.

Blair's cheeks pinkened and her little lips quivered when she seemed to notice her father's distress.

"There, there," Forres shushed the babe.

"She's fine, truly. I was able to catch her before she fell in," Rowena assured him.

"Fell in?" Clear eyes, gray as a winter's sky, met hers. A tremor rippled through her. How had she forgotten what looking at him made her feel? Dizzy, excited, and a little anxious. Of course, last night they'd had a dozen people between them, and all manner of candles, dishes, and other things to block them from speaking directly. Yet there had been one moment, when he'd joined in the toasting for the evening and he'd raised his glass. His eyes had traveled from face to face, lingering only on hers.

"Yes, she was climbing onto the edge of the fountain when I found her."

"Good God," he muttered. "I only knew she'd wandered away from the nursery." He gave Blair a kiss on her forehead before looking toward Rowena.

He combed his fingers through hair that was a little too

long for the current fashion. There was something different about him, as though the suit he wore was a costume. With his broad shoulders, great height, and muscled form, he was more fit for the role of a Scottish warrior of old than a gentleman in a garden. The thought of him in a kilt, brandishing a sword, like a man out of her deepest, secret dreams... another shiver rippled through her and she swallowed hard. She was still young enough to have silly daydreams about handsome lords whisking her away to castles.

"Thank you, Miss Rowena. I apologize for my...harsh reaction." Forres gripped little Blair's head gently with one strong hand as he clutched his daughter to his chest. He closed his eyes and nuzzled her soft curls.

"No need to apologize," Rowena said. She smoothed out her skirts, feeling a little embarrassed at witnessing such a strong show of emotion from a man who the nurse had said guarded his heart.

Forres met her gaze. "I went to check on Blair and when she was gone, I panicked...A footman said he thought he'd seen her leave the house." He shook his head as though to banish dark thoughts. "I'm just glad she's all right."

"'Course she is, my lord. The young lady caught her right quick. The wee bairn was safe in her care," Mrs. Finch told Lord Forres.

"Why don't I take the lass inside for a bite to eat and a

nap?" Mrs. Finch reached for Blair, but Forres didn't immediately hand his daughter over. When he finally did, it was with a sigh and great reluctance.

"Be a good girl, Blair." He chucked her under the chin and the little girl bobbled up and down in her nurse's arms.

Rowena watched this familial intimacy, her heart flipping inside her chest. Mrs. Finch started to walk back toward the main house, and as she passed by Rowena, Blair reached out with one chubby little hand and waved at her before resting her cheek on Mrs. Finch's shoulder. A strange pull in her made her want to rush after the child.

The Earl of Forres cleared his throat and Rowena came back to herself.

"Have you been enjoying the house party, Lord Forres?" she asked, hoping that was the right course of conversation. It was the first time she'd been alone with a man besides her father or servants.

Alone with a man...

Rowena's heart tripped and she had to collect herself before she panicked. Her sister Milly had just gotten engaged early this morning, against her will, because a fortune hunter had snuck into her room the previous night and been caught by their mother. Nothing beyond that had happened, but it had been enough to scandalize them into marriage. Was being alone with Forres like this enough for a scandal?

"The party has been a pleasant distraction," Forres admitted.

She nodded. "Yes." She swallowed. Why was she so nervous? Normally she loved conversation and could talk about almost anything. Being alone with him left her tongue-tied and tingling as he drew near.

He held out the crook of his arm in silent invitation. The gesture was gentlemanly, but also natural and masculine.

The heat of a blush worked its way to her cheeks and Rowena didn't know what to do.

"Oh, come now, Miss Rowena, 'tis only my arm. I won't bite." He grinned at her and chomped his white teeth together in a mocking way.

A giggle escaped her, startling them both. Then he laughed, too, but there was a surprise in his expression as though he was astounded at his own amusement. The sound of his laugh was rich and warm and oddly comforting, given that he was a complete stranger. After only a brief hesitation, she placed her arm in his. Little tingles shot up her skin at the point of their connection.

"Allow me to escort you back to the house." Forres nodded toward the massive tan stone edifice of Hampton House. It reminded her so much of Pepperwirth Vale, her family estate only four miles away. Two ancient families, the Grahams and the Pepperwirths, had been neighbors for nearly two hundred years.

She and Forres walked in silence for a few steps before Forres spoke.

"I wish to thank you again for rescuing my daughter. Blair is..." He paused, and Rowena peeked up at him, noticing a slight ruddiness to his cheeks. "Blair is very precious to me. I'm afraid I'm overly protective of her."

"I understand, my lord. I was informed you'd lost your wife a year ago, my condolences. It must be hard for any parent to raise a child alone."

Forres halted and turned to face her, his eyes slightly wide in surprise. "Yes...yes, it is hard." He recovered himself. "Blair is a wee bit wild, as I was when I was a bairn."

Rowena couldn't resist smiling. "You were once a wee child?" Her own childhood had been full of adventures, as much as a well-bred English young lady could have had in the country, but she imagined Forres had a much more colorful life.

"Oh, aye..." His Scottish accent thickened to a richer brogue as he spoke. "I was always off in the woods or on a horse. My nurse couldn't keep me in a clean set of trousers to save my life." His solemn gray eyes held a hint of warmth as he led her through the maze of gardens.

"And little Blair is like you." Rowena laughed in

delight. The idea of the darling child running among the Scottish heather, wild and free, was a wonderful thought.

Forres nodded. "Yes, but she could use a wee bit of taming."

"Taming?" Rowena asked, tempted to smile. "All children need to be able to run free sometimes. I was often getting into scrapes when I was younger."

Forres gazed at her. "Now, that I cannot imagine! A proper young lady like you?" His expression was serious but there was a hint of gentle mocking in his tone. He was teasing her and she couldn't help but grin at him, temporarily forgetting how nervous he made her.

"Oh yes, I was a bit of a tree climber and I was always bringing home tadpoles, baby birds, and all other manner of fauna. I once nursed a baby deer back to health after its mother was killed one spring." She'd always loved taking care of wounded creatures great or small, and her parents had been thankfully indulgent of her desire to play the healer.

He covered her hand with his where it rested on his arm. "I was much the same. Always bringing home creatures. I rescued a pine marten one winter, raising the kit in my bedchamber beneath my parents' noses. It was a fine beast, a smart creature. He lived for nine years as a devoted pet, much to my mother's dismay."

"It must have been wonderful to grow up in a castle in

Scotland as a child." Rowena sighed dreamily, picturing the earl as a boy scampering about the woods.

"It was, but southern England here is just as beautiful. You live on the neighboring estate, don't you?"

"Yes, Pepperwirth Vale. It is a lovely house and all my memories there are happy ones." She was beginning to see just how fortunate she had been to grow up so loved and cherished and free of tragedy.

Before they could speak further, they'd reached the doors to the veranda at the back of Hampton House, and Rowena's mother was rushing toward her. Her mother, usually one to be immaculately dressed, was now wearing a wrinkled gown, her hair a bit frazzled. She must have been up all night worrying about Milly's situation.

"Rowena! Dear, you must come at once, your sister..." Her mother halted at the sight of Lord Forres standing beside Rowena, their arms still linked.

"Lord Forres." Lady Pepperwirth recovered, her strained features smoothing into a beautiful mask of pleasantry.

"Good morning, Lady Pepperwirth." Forres bowed.

"Er...yes, good morning, my lord. I'm so sorry for disrupting your walk with my daughter." Her gaze darted between them.

Forres seemed to sense her unease, and ever the gentleman, he took control of the situation.

"Shall I go speak with the staff regarding luncheon?"

"Oh yes, thank you, Lord Forres," Lady Pepperwirth exclaimed in relief.

Forres turned his focus to Rowena and heat flooded her cheeks when he took the hand that had been resting upon his arm and pressed a lingering kiss on her bare skin. When he released her hand, Rowena clutched it to her chest as she watched the handsome Scotsman stride away into the house.

"Well, that's certainly encouraging, isn't it?" Her mother glanced back at where Forres had gone.

With a little exasperated sigh, Rowena stared at her mother.

"He is very polite, Mama, but I don't think—"

"Oh hush, every man with good sense would be interested in you, dear. From the moment you were born, I knew you would grow up to be a beauty, just like your sister, but thank heavens you've a sweeter temperament."

"Mama!" Rowena protested. "You know Milly is as sweet as me. She simply doesn't suffer fools." Rowena adored her older sister but sometimes Milly acted a bit prickly, especially to young men, because she feared marriage and the loss of her sense of self. It was a complicated notion, but Rowena understood that Milly feared a husband would repress her freedom.

Lady Pepperwirth puffed out her chest. "Yes, well, your sister has certainly gotten herself involved in a bit of trouble with her attitude. Your father and I have a fine mess to deal with getting a wedding arranged quickly with as little scandal as possible."

Guilt clawed at Rowena's insides and she pressed a hand to her stomach. Here she had been enjoying a walk with Lord Forres while her sister was no doubt suffering preparations for a wedding to a man she didn't know and didn't love.

It was my fault she was compromised. That part made Rowena feel even worse. The previous evening Milly had come to her and explained that she was worried that Owen Hadley, the handsome fortune hunter, had set his sights on Rowena. Unfortunately, Milly had been right about Owen and had been compromised when he'd snuck into her room by accident. It was their wedding her parents now had to plan.

"Does she really have to marry him?" The thought of her beloved sister trapped into a marriage because she'd been protecting Rowena...It made Rowena's stomach roll over.

"Of course she does," her mother said with a slight frown. "But don't worry about her, Rowena; she can use a bit of marriage to improve her mood. Mr. Hadley might be a suitable match after all. Now come, dear, tell me how you and Lord Forres met this morning."

Rowena rolled her eyes. Her mother was relentless when it came to marrying off her children. Unfortunately for her, Rowena wanted a love match.

"I don't think he is interested in me, Mama. He was being polite; that is all."

"Humph," her mother huffed. "Well, his land holdings in Forres are immense, his temperament is good, and he's a fine-looking man. We'd best snap him up before he takes his wife hunting to London."

Snap him up? That was the last thing she needed. A husband. Of course she wanted one, but she'd only just come out. A girl had every right to embrace the freedom of the city in the late fall, the dancing, the balls, the gowns, the suitors...Rowena did want to experience it at least once before she made a decision.

"Mama, I want to enjoy the Season. Must we discuss marriage *now*?" She knew she sounded a little childish, but she didn't want to rush such a monumental decision.

"Well, I suppose we have plenty of time to discuss Lord Forres later." Her mother's lips pursed. "I've come to tell you that your father and I must take Milly straight home to settle the wedding plans. You are to remain here at Hampton for the duration of the party. The dowager countess will be a diligent chaperone for you."

Her parents were leaving? Rowena clutched her mother's arm. "But you can't go, Mama. I need you here—"

"Nonsense. It's time you were off my leading strings and on your own for a bit. We won't be far." Lady Pepperwirth patted her hand gently.

Following her inside the grand Hampton House,

Rowena paused in the entry. The muted gold light coming in through the vast windows illuminated the grand staircase. Only last night she'd descended those steps as a debutante in a white gown, the eyes of every man at the party fixed on her. She didn't revel in the attention, but it was pleasant to be noticed for once.

But the night was over, today was a new day, and she wondered what she was supposed to do without her mother or her sister here to guide her. Dinner was easy enough, discussions, courses of the meal, she'd learned it all, but...what was she to do during the day on her own?

"Oh, Milly, I wish I were you," Rowena murmured. "You'd know exactly what to do."

Chapter 2

Quinn MacCauley, the seventh earl of Forres, stared out of the wide French windows facing the veranda of Hampton House. The midmorning tea had just been laid out and a light luncheon was being prepared. Yet Quinn could not focus on these details. His mind, as it was wont to do this last year, drifted.

The ring finger on his left hand was bare, and he felt naked without the silver band he'd worn until a month ago.

Sweet Maura...

Had it truly been a year since his wife had died giving birth to the baby boy that had perished with her? He didn't feel ready to move on—he doubted he ever would —but Blair, his darling, wee bairn, needed a mother. She was growing up so fast, and before he knew it she'd be presented at court and suitors would be knocking at his door. As a single father, he feared he'd closet Blair away in a tower and not let her live a full life. It would happen all too soon, and knowing that made him hurt deep inside with a heavy ache of loneliness.

It was all of this that had him traipsing through England on a wife hunt. Any Scottish lass would have been fine, but he feared they would remind him of Maura. So he and Mrs. Finch had taken Blair and left Forres to come to England to find a woman.

He didn't expect to fall in love again, not after how he'd loved Maura. She was his childhood sweetheart, his dearest friend, his lover. The woman he'd chased through the wild heather and rode out on the grounds with every morning. The gaping hole in his heart was still raw. Absently, he rubbed his bare ring finger again as he watched Leo Graham, the Earl of Hampton, and his fiancée, Ivy Leighton, walk into the dining room. Their heads were bent toward one another as they shared whispers and secret smiles. The ache in his chest grew.

Ivy and Leo paused when they noticed him standing beside the windows.

"Forres! How the devil are you?" Leo beamed and strode over to Quinn, Ivy at his side.

"Good, Hampton. And you?" They'd only had a brief

moment at dinner the previous evening to exchange greetings.

"Good." Leo smiled. "I'm delighted Mother thought to invite you down to the house for a few weeks before you travel to London."

Quinn nodded. "Aye, 'twas good of her to think of me." Leo's mother, the dowager countess, was a distant cousin of his. The convoluted bloodlines of the English and the Scots left him well connected to many of London's titled elite, including the Grahams.

"Well, seems like it will be just us for lunch. Mother isn't feeling too well, and the Pepperwirths are going home early. Hadley's leaving too; apparently we're to congratulate him on a wedding he needs to plan." Leo's lips twitched and Quinn sensed there was more to this situation than was being revealed, but he knew better than to pry.

"Oh, but, Leo, don't forget, Rowena is staying." Ivy nudged Leo in the ribs, her eyes darting between him and Quinn suggestively.

Leo's eyes widened as if finally reading his fiancée's thoughts, and then he coughed. "Er...yes, Rowena. You've met Miss Rowena, haven't you, Forres?"

Quinn nodded, amused that the couple in front of him seemed to be planning some attempt at matchmaking. Despite his heartache, he was finding the general hunt for a wife to be humorous. It was either laugh at his situation or cry, and he was not going to cry. He had shed his tears and was now determined to do what he needed to do for Blair.

As a Scot, he was a fair outsider to the English aristocracy's eccentricities with regard to courtship and marriage. Last night during dinner he'd watched the women in the room eye him appraisingly, and rather than be offended, he was surprised at how much it entertained him. The language of soft smiles and suggestive questions they posed to him, as though assessing his prospects for themselves or their daughters, had been amusing. And he had been just as interested in them for the same reason, attempting to see if any might prove a good match. But none at dinner had truly attracted him in the end. None except Rowena.

He couldn't help but rub his bare finger again as he thought of Rowena rescuing Blair from falling into the fountain. She'd saved his child and he wasn't going to forget that any time soon.

"Why don't you fetch her for luncheon, Lord Forres," Ivy suggested to him.

"I'd be happy to." Quinn nodded at them both. They were an attractive couple, Leo with his fair features and Ivy with her dark hair and olive skin. Like the sun and moon.

"Pardon me." Quinn left the dining room and walked down the corridor until he reached the main hall, where he froze, arrested by the sight of a woman alone by the stairs.

Rowena Pepperwirth stood directly in the path of a wide beam of sunlight coming through the high windows. Her pale gold hair glinted and shimmered like silk in the light. Her elaborate coiffure, with its coiled lengths done up in an artfully messy style, was so unlike the way Maura had worn her reddish brown hair. Quinn shook his head, banishing the comparison. They were different women and he should not compare her to his wife. He did not want a woman to replace Maura; he wanted someone new, someone who was her own woman.

"Oh, Milly." The young woman sighed. "I wish you were here; you'd know exactly what to do." Her voice was soft, a little husky, more womanly than girlish. She was young, a new debutante, but Rowena was a lovely woman coming into her own.

A little smiled curved Quinn's mouth up. She was more than lovely; she was exquisite. Her body was small in stature but with healthy curves. Rowena, at only eighteen, was perhaps naïve of the world, but she had been good with Blair. Natural mothering instincts. She'd make any man a fine wife...Quinn suddenly tensed as that thought occurred to him. That was not something he could just ignore, being as he was on the hunt for exactly that.

Leaning his shoulder against the wall, he studied her more closely. The white lace day gown she wore was dotted with smudges of dirt near her knees...where she'd leaned over the stone fountain to catch his daughter. A pink blush heightened the color in her cheeks as she wrung her hands, still talking to herself under her breath.

A few wisps of her hair came loose from the coiffure and dangled down her neck. An unexpected heated interest flooded his body as he pictured himself standing directly behind her, hands on her hips as he bent to nibble and kiss that neck. She would smell sweet, like rosewater, and her laugh as he kissed her would be breathless and husky. She would turn and curl her arms around his neck...Quinn blinked, shocked that he'd been lost in such thoughts. He hadn't felt attraction to any woman since Maura.

A moment later guilt followed and he ducked his head, drew a steadying breath, and focused on Rowena again. His primary hunt for a wife so far had been to study women with regard to their ability to be good mothers, but seeing Rowena now...it reminded him that any wife he took would also be his lover, not merely a mother to his children. It was a truth he could not ignore. He had been celibate since Maura died, but if he married again, especially if he took a woman like Rowena to wife, he would need to—would want to—consummate the marriage. Again that sense of guilt crawled beneath his skin.

Maura is gone, he reminded himself. Many widowers

moved on to new wives, but Quinn was finding it hard to imagine loving any other woman ever again.

I don't have to love her, but I can have an affection for her, enjoy her in my bed, can't I?

He regained his control and cleared his throat. Rowena jumped and whirled to face him.

"Lord Forres!" she gasped. "You startled me!"

He tried to calm her with a wave of his hand. The panic in her cornflower-blue eyes was something he regretted causing. He left the doorway to come over to her.

"I'm sorry, Miss Rowena. I came to fetch you for luncheon if you're ready." He crooked his arm, and, as he had in the garden earlier, after a brief hesitation, she placed her hand through it. It was a simple touch, nothing at all romantic in it—it wasn't as though he were pinning her against the wall and kissing her—yet he felt a forbidden thrill each time his and Rowena's bodies came into contact, even as innocently as this.

A strange stirring filled his chest. It was a curious sensation, one he had not felt since...since Blair had been born. Only then did Quinn recognize what it was: a nervous excitement. How odd that this young woman he barely knew could make him feel as such. It had been months since he'd felt much of anything. Only Blair brought him any joy.

"Do we...er..." Rowena nibbled her plump bottom lip

as though embarrassed to speak. He tried not to focus on her lips or how he had the sudden urge to nip them.

"What I meant to say is, do we have plans this afternoon?" Rowena ducked her head as she added, "This is my first house party and with my parents gone, I'm a little..."

"Out of your depth?" Quinn smiled. "I know exactly how you feel. A Scotsman doesn't always feel he is on steady ground once he crosses the border into England." He kept his tone light, teasing, and it earned a laugh from Rowena. The sound was musical, full of joy and relief. This fair English rose was an open creature, emotions plain upon her delicate features, and her eyes, such blue eyes that made a man thirsty to gaze upon, hid nothing of what was in her mind and heart.

"Thank heavens for that, my lord. I must admit, I'm nervous I will make a ninny of myself whilst my parents are gone." Her gentle, concerned confession tugged at his heart. The organ, so hardened into stone over the last year, jolted with an unexpected pulse.

"Do not worry, Miss Rowena, we shall survive the party together. At least today it shall be just us with Hampton and his bride-to-be. Four is not too intimidating a size for an afternoon." He almost covered her hand with his but caught himself. *I must behave. I cannot do more than offer my arm to her.*

"That is a relief. Leo, er...that is to say, Lord Hampton

is such a dear. And so is Ivy." Then her face turned a bright scarlet. "I ought not to call them that. I keep forgetting. Mama would be furious if she caught me not using titles. I always forget when it comes to my friends." She laughed at herself.

And there it was. That glimpse of who this woman was inside. A woman with a heart so open to friendliness and joy that she often called her friends by their Christian names. This was not the sort of woman he would find in London among the balls, dinners, and other engagements. Rowena was a rare and extraordinary creature.

"If that is the case, I'd much prefer if you called me Quinn. I, too, am not inclined toward formality when I can help it." A silly grin stretched his lips; he couldn't stop it. There was something about Rowena that caught him off guard and he relaxed around her.

Her blue eyes twinkled like the noon sunlight upon a loch's surface, sparkling with a kaleidoscope of colors.

"Then I will be Rowena to you," she replied, the red blush still staining her cheeks. "Oh look! Luncheon!" She nodded at the elegant setting as they entered the dining room.

The long mahogany table in the center of the room was set for only four places near the far end. A matching end piece sat against one wall, laden with dishes of cold turkey, lamb, pigeon, cold pie and ptarmigan, puddings, cheeses, biscuits, jellies, and fruit ready to be served. The soft pale green walls were decorated with portraits of the Hampton ancestors, who peered down at them from layers of oil.

Ivy and Leo were already serving themselves on small plates. A footman stood in the corner of the room, ready to assist if necessary. Ivy smoothed her bright blue tea gown with one hand as she saw them come in, and she broke into a wide smile.

"Rowena, come sit by me." Ivy patted the chair beside her.

Quinn kept his hold on Rowena's arm and walked over to the chair beside Ivy; then he released her in order to pull the chair back. Once she was seated, he leaned over a little, catching the hint of rosewater perfume she wore. Just like he'd imagined...

"Allow me to bring you a plate," he murmured.

Rowena glanced up at him, her eyes wide and delighted. "Thank you, Quinn." His name came off her lips so naturally, and his body warmed at simply hearing it.

Joining Leo at the side table, he fixed two plates, one for himself and one for Rowena, before he and Leo took their seats at the table.

"Now," Leo began with an amused glint in his eyes, "Ivy has just reminded me there is a wonderful old set of ruins we could ride up to and have a look around."

Quinn blinked. "Are you sure? It looks like rain." When he'd rushed out to the gardens earlier, he'd scented it upon the air. That crisp, clear aroma was unmistakably rain. White clouds hung low upon the distant horizon, but they weren't dark yet. Still, he knew when a storm was coming. It was a skill he'd attributed to living a life out of doors upon his estate at Forres. If there was one thing he knew about the English, it was that they played at being outdoorsmen, but most were too used to their pampered life of aristocratic splendor.

Scotland was harsh at times, the winters colder, the land less inclined to yield food. It made men stronger, and the women too. He glanced at Rowena again. Perhaps he was wrong to seek an English bride, one who was not used to such harsh environments. But the thought of hearing his name uttered in a familiar Scottish tongue and not have it be from Maura's lips...he could not bear it. No, better he marry an English lass because she would not remind him of what he'd lost. Again he stilled as he realized he was considering Rowena among his bridal prospects. But why shouldn't he? She was young, beautiful, sweet with Blair, intelligent...

"We'll take the Stanley. If it starts to rain, we can drive back. What do you say, Forres?"

With a shrug, Quinn settled in to eat his luncheon. "If the ladies wish to go, I'm happy to oblige."

"It does sound fun." Rowena grinned happily across the table at him. Her smile was infectious.

When he reached for the buttered toast, he noticed Ivy

was watching him, an intense but not unfriendly focus gleaming in her warm, dark eyes. He offered her a small smile, which she returned before focusing on Leo.

After the luncheon was over, the four of them retired to their chambers in order to dress more warmly for their outing. Quinn paused before the mirror close to his bed as he slid on his Chesterfield, a single-breasted coat of herringbone tweed. The velvet collar of the coat would keep his neck warm in case it did rain and a chill set in. His valet helped him tidy up his clothes before he exited his chambers. Hampton was just leaving his room and they descended the grand staircase together.

"Hampton, what do think of Miss Rowena?" Quinn slid his black leather gloves on as they reached the bottom stair.

Leo dug around in his coat until he found his own gloves. With a covert glance about the main hall, Leo leaned close to him.

"She's a lovely young woman, only just come out. Her presentation caused quite a stir in London. I imagine she won't be on the market long." Leo shot him a sideways glance as he propped one arm against the banister railing. "Mother thought you might be wife hunting. Is that true, Forres?"

Rather than be angered by the blunt question, he was amused at the thought of his intentions being uncovered by Leo's mother. She was undoubtedly shrewd.

"Truth be told, I am. Blair needs a mother and the running of my household has become a burden I would be glad to share with a wife." Since Maura had died, his sister had assumed the role, but Quinn was not blind. He'd seen Kenna mooning over wedding dresses in her fashion magazines from Paris and getting lost in daydreams of her own life. She deserved to have a chance to live and not suffer under any obligations Maura's death may have left her with. Therefore, Quinn *needed* a wife.

"Well, then," Leo chuckled, "Rowena would suit you very well. She's been trained to care for a large household, and I daresay she is affable too. But..." Leo paused, his eyes narrowing in speculation.

"But?" Quinn pressed.

Leo looked heavenward and sighed. "She's a romantic and a dreamer, Forres. If I have learned anything from Ivy, it's that you must let a woman be who she is meant to be. No clipping their wings, no binding them in marital shackles that would crush their spirits. The women of today are not like our mothers. They believe in equality and marriage as partnerships. Rowena is young but she'll be like her sister, opinionated and intelligent."

Quinn considered this and did not find fault with the idea. "A woman who knows her own mind is not a bad thing."

"Agreed," Leo said. "Rowena's natural sweetness hides

much, but do not be fooled. She will wish to run her own life as much as you do yours."

Quinn stared at Leo. Never had an Englishman been so frank with him before.

"Your observations are noted, Hampton. I'll be wise to remember your advice." He lowered his voice as he glimpsed a flutter of skirts at the top of the stairs.

Ivy appeared first, her lavender day gown with black trim a complement to her dark hair and olive-skinned complexion. She was hastily buttoning up a woolen overcoat. Quinn's eyes moved from her and all thoughts of Ivy and her loveliness were eclipsed when he caught a glimpse of Rowena.

He swallowed hard, strangely unable to speak as she descended the stairs. She wore a golden yellow gown, almost a rich mustard color, embroidered with red leaves on the hem and sleeves. Rather than wear a coat, she carried a gray plaid cape. Like a ray of sunlight, she seemed to float down the stairs in a brilliant splash of color. It took a moment for him to catch his breath.

"Do I look all right, Quinn?" She was staring down at herself in concern.

"Beg pardon?" Quinn finally got out as Rowena paused two steps above him. It placed her directly at eye level with him. He couldn't help but gaze at her rosy lips.

"You're staring, old boy," Leo muttered in his ear.

With a little jerk, Quinn uttered an apology. Rowena dropped his chin, her cheeks red.

"Let me." He reached for her cloak and she turned her back, letting him drape it around her shoulders.

"The Stanley is ready," Leo announced.

The group proceeded to the main door, which the butler opened. Leo escorted Ivy to the car.

"Quinn, do you mind sitting in the back with Miss Rowena?" he asked.

Sit next to a lovely woman? If he ever woke up one morning and answered no to that question, there was definitely something wrong with him.

"I'd be happy to," Quinn answered as he took charge of Rowena and lifted her up into the car's backseat. He was presented with a glimpse of her bottom, all too tempting, even covered by the bright yellow gown. A flare of unexpected arousal hit him like a bolt of lightning.

Must bury it deep. Quinn clenched his jaw and climbed into the car behind Rowena. He could survive one bloody afternoon, couldn't he?

About the Author

USA TODAY Bestselling Author Lauren Smith is an Oklahoma attorney by day, who pens adventurous and edgy romance stories by the light of her smart phone flashlight app. She knew she was destined to be a romance writer when she attempted to re-write the entire *Titanic* movie just to save Jack from drowning. Connecting with readers by writing emotionally moving, realistic and sexy romances no matter what time period is her passion. She's won multiple awards in several romance subgenres including: New England Reader's Choice Awards, Greater Detroit BookSeller's Best Awards, and a Semi-Finalist award for the Mary Wollstonecraft Shelley Award.

To connect with Lauren, visit her at:

www.laurensmithbooks.com

lauren@Laurensmithbooks.com

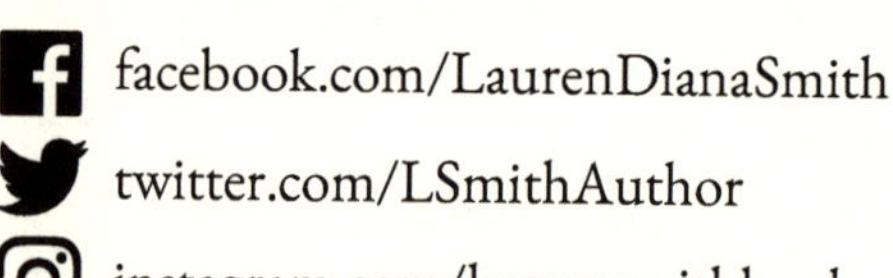
facebook.com/LaurenDianaSmith
twitter.com/LSmithAuthor
instagram.com/laurensmithbooks

Made in the USA
Columbia, SC
19 November 2023

26773280R00167